"You're not going to share what you've discovered, are you?"

"Don't take it personally, Liana. I realize that it involves your husband, but it's also a police investigation. I fully intend to charge someone for Billy's murder, and because of that, I can't share every bit of the case with you. It could jeopardize it."

"I see." Even though his words made sense, she felt betrayed.

He still looked worried. "Does that mean you understand?"

"Not exactly. It means I understand that there's not a lot I can do right now. I wish there was."

He reached out for her hand. "You could hold my hand. You could try to trust me."

She linked her fingers through his and smiled.

But all she could think was that Kent was going to have to trust her one day. She was going to have to try to trust him, too.

Liana wondered if that was even possible.

Shelley Shepard Gray writes inspirational and sweet contemporary romances for a variety of publishers. With over a million books in print, and translated into more than a dozen languages, her novels have reached both the *New York Times* and the *USA TODAY* bestseller lists. Shelley's novels have also been featured in a variety of national publications.

In addition to her writing, Shelley has hosted several well-attended Girlfriend Getaways for Amish reading fans. Her most recent Girlfriend Getaway, hosted with several other novelists, was highlighted on Netflix's *Follow This* series.

Before writing romances, Shelley taught school and earned her bachelor's degree in English literature and later obtained her master's degree in educational administration. She now lives in southern Colorado near her grown children, walks her dachshunds, bakes too much and writes full-time.

ʒ

WIDOW'S SECRETS

SHELLEY SHEPARD GRAY

LOVE INSPIRED
INSPIRATIONAL ROMANCE

LOVE INSPIRED®
INSPIRATIONAL ROMANCE

ISBN-13: 978-1-335-63339-2

Widow's Secrets

Copyright © 2021 by Shelley Sabga

This edition published by arrangement with Harlequin Books S.A.

For questions and comments about the quality of this book, please contact us at CustomerService@Harlequin.com.

Love Inspired
22 Adelaide St. West, 40th Floor
Toronto, Ontario M5H 4E3, Canada
www.Harlequin.com

Printed in U.S.A.

I acknowledged my sin unto thee,
and mine iniquity have I not hid. I said,
I will confess my transgressions unto the Lord;
and thou forgavest the iniquity of my sin.
—*Psalm* 32:5

Opportunities are never lost.
Someone will always take the ones you miss.
—Amish Proverb

For Johanna Raisanen and Kathleen Scheibling,
two ladies who've proved that it really is possible
to have lasting relationships in publishing.

Acknowledgments

I'm so grateful to the many people who helped
make this novel a reality. First my thanks goes to
editors Kathleen Scheibling and Johanna Raisanen,
who tweeted about a new Cold Case series
and then so kindly answered my emails when
I wasn't even sure if they remembered who I was.
Both ladies were encouraging and so helpful
during this whole process.

I'm also indebted to my agent, Nicole Resciniti,
of the Seymour Agency. Nicole was nothing but
supportive when I told her about my wish to
contribute to this series.

Thanks also to Lynne Stroup, who quickly read
both my proposal and the first draft and offered
many suggestions to make the book better.

Finally, I must give a shout-out to my Harlequin
writer friends, who were so kind to offer their
congrats and support to me. Their friendship
brought a lot of smiles during a stressful year.

Officer Grune stepped forward, almost edging the detective off her small cement stoop. "We have some news to share with you, Liana. May we come in?"

Ten years ago she used to try to be polite. She would shake the police officers' hands and invite them in. One time she'd even served everyone coffee, like she was the type of woman who entertained guests all the time.

Now, because she knew that she never had a choice, Liana just stepped back so they could walk inside.

Detective Evans led the way into the living room but didn't sit down. Instead, he was looking around the dark room in a confused way.

Liana knew why. All the lights in the house were off. Though she hadn't intended to say a word about it, she apologized as she turned on one of the lights. "Sorry. I'm afraid my Amish neighbors have rubbed off on me." When the detective still looked confused, she explained, "They don't have electricity, you know."

"Oh. Yeah." He cleared his throat. "Can we sit down? This won't take long."

"Of course." She gestured to the lumpy couch. The three of them could squeeze next to each other there for all she cared. She took the wooden rocking chair in the corner.

To her amusement, only the detective and Libby sat down. Officer Silverstone, after looking at the small amount of available space, stood against the wall.

After another moment of uncomfortable silence, Detective Evans pulled out a notepad and scanned it. Then he gazed at her directly. "Mrs. Mann, the body of an adult man was found in a crevice about fifteen miles from here. After recovering the remains, our lab con-

Prologue

Seven months ago

The moment Liana saw the two police cruisers park in front of her house, she'd known whatever they intended to say was going to be bad. Glad that her hands and T-shirt were clean—she'd been painting in her studio all morning—she opened the door before any of the three officers could knock. She'd grown to hate the sound of fists pounding against wood.

"Yes?" she asked.

The officer who was in the front—a slim man in a blazer, slacks and polished black shoes—paused before regaining his composure. "Mrs. Mann, I don't know if you remember me. I'm Detective Doug Evans." He held out a hand.

She didn't shake it, just gripped the door frame mor tightly. "I remember you."

He paused again. "This is Officer Silverstone. I lieve you know Officer Grune, as well?"

"Yes." Officer Libby Grune had interviewed he eral times when Billy had first gone missing.

ducted DNA tests. I regret to inform you that your husband was a match."

"You found Billy."

"Well, we found Billy's remains," Officer Silverstone blurted.

Liana lifted her gaze. The young officer's cheeks were stained with embarrassment. After steadying herself, she asked, "How did my husband die? Do you know that?"

"We're pretty certain he was murdered, ma'am," Officer Silverstone murmured. "I'm very sorry."

"I see."

The silence continued.

Looking pained, Libby leaned forward. "I'm sorry for your loss, Liana. I know your husband has been gone for some time, but this still has to be difficult to hear."

Liana wasn't sure if this news was *difficult* or not. Living with Billy had been difficult. Having him go missing and then being subjected to weeks and weeks of questioning had been difficult. Spending ten years wondering if she was a widow or not had been really hard, too. Wondering whether Billy would one day show up out of the blue and expect her to take him right back had almost been her undoing.

But this? Well, she wasn't sure what *this* was.

"What do you need me to do?" she asked.

Detective Evans blinked. "Do you have any questions, Mrs. Mann?"

Only one. "Do you know who murdered him?"

"Not yet."

"We think Billy was likely killed ten years ago,

Liana," Libby said, her voice quietly compassionate. "My guess is it happened soon after he went missing."

They didn't know who killed her husband. It was likely that they never would. Surely, there wasn't anything more to say.

Ready to regain her privacy, she stood up. "Thank you all for coming to tell me the news." She walked to the front door and opened it.

The brisk October breeze blew inside, chilling the temperature of the room. Detective Evans pulled out a card and handed it to her. "Here's my contact information if you need it. In the meantime someone will be calling to discuss what you'd like to do next."

With Billy's body. That was what he was referring to. "All right." She took the card and slid it into the back pocket of her jeans.

After Detective Evans walked out the door, followed by Officer Silverstone, Officer Grune paused in front of her. "Again, I'm sorry for your loss, Liana," she said, handing Liana another card. "If you, ah, have any further questions or concerns, don't hesitate to reach out."

"Thank you," she said as the woman followed the men down the narrow path to their cars.

The moment they opened their vehicles' doors, Liana closed hers. Then she clicked the dead bolt.

And then she slid down on the floor and rested her head against the cold wood.

Billy was dead. He wasn't going to come back. Not ever.

There would be no more panic attacks at two in the morning as she contemplated what would happen when he returned. No more living in limbo as both a wife and a widow. No more bruises on her face or arms or side or thighs to either shake off or cover up.

That long, exhausting period of her life was all over. It was just too bad that it had taken ten years.

Chapter One

❧

Monday, May 4

"You want to take that one or should I?" Angel asked as Chris Pine's look-alike walked through the diner's front door. "He's a regular snack." She grinned. "Right?"

"I will," Liana said, barely refraining from rolling her eyes. From the day Angel had started at Dig In Diner, the girl had been a stereotype old-school waitress come to life.

She wore it well, too. Angel had bleached-blond hair and an enviable figure encased in a uniform that was one size too small, cracked a constant wad of gum and treated everyone to big, bright smiles. Everybody loved the girl, Liana included. She only wished that Angel would stop referring to half-decent-looking men like tasty treats.

"I don't blame you for wanting that one. Well, go get 'em, Tiger." Angel laughed before walking in the opposite direction.

The man, all blue eyes and perfect physique encased in faded denim and a gray T-shirt, looked a little wary

He also had a pad of paper and a pencil in front of him.

She sat down on the red vinyl bench across from him. "I only have a few minutes."

His expression warmed, as though her crankiness amused him. "All right, then. My name is Kent Olson. I was recently assigned to investigate some cold cases in the region. I decided to focus on your husband."

Billy. Her mouth went dry. "Billy died ten years ago, Officer."

"And his body was discovered about seven months ago." He picked up his pencil, seeming certain Liana had a lot to say.

She did not. Now that she finally had closure, she had done everything she possibly could to remove him from her life. There was nothing about Billy Mann that she wanted to revisit.

"I cooperated with everyone both times. I told the officers everything I knew," she said quietly. Well, what she'd ever intended to share. What she didn't mention was that she hadn't known much about her husband's private life at all. Billy had enjoyed keeping secrets and she'd gotten really good at pretending they didn't exist.

Officer Olson fussed with the pencil, tapping the eraser end against the table. "We did an autopsy. His neck was broken and the medical examiner found traces of ligature marks on his throat."

"Ligature marks?"

"As if he'd been strangled." He paused. "Although we didn't find a bullet, the medical examiner also believes he was shot. Did you know that?"

"Yes." Even to her ears, her voice sounded rough. When his eyebrows rose, she tried to explain her reaction. "When Detective Evans and Officer Grune came to see me, I… I'm afraid everything was a blur. I don't remember many of the details."

"Not even about his murder?"

Looking at him in the eye, she shrugged. "I thought it was over." It was a poor answer but it was actually the truth. All she'd ever cared about was that Billy wasn't coming back into her life.

Instead of questioning her some more, he looked satisfied by that, like she'd passed a test Liana hadn't even known about. After scribbling something on that pad of paper, Officer Olson leaned back against the bench. "I think we have a lot to talk about, Ms. Mann. I want to know more about your husband. Look around your property."

"He's been gone ten years."

"Yes, but since you still live in the same house, it's important to me." His expression hardened along with his voice. "Discovering what happened to Billy Mann is important to me, ma'am."

"Here's your order," Viv announced, her voice hard. "You might want to eat before it gets cold, sir."

That was all the incentive Liana needed to get to her feet. "I'll go fetch you some more coffee."

Turning away, she kept her head down, avoiding eye contact with Viv as she grabbed a carafe. Her insides felt like black tar had coated them, making every bit of her feel uncomfortable and poisoned.

She was going to need to start praying again—and start trying to figure out how she was going to survive this next round of questions.

One step at a time, she reminded herself. That was all she had to do—stop thinking about the future and the past and only concentrate on each minute, then hour, of the day. That was the way to survive.

Billy had taught her that.

Officer Olson was writing notes with one hand and holding a piece of bacon with the other when she approached again. "More coffee?"

"Yeah. Thanks." While she poured, he slid a white business card toward her. "Ms. Mann, here's my contact information. You need to call and set up our next meeting. Soon. Otherwise, I'll be forced to stop by here again."

That sounded like a threat. Years ago she might have called him on that. Might have even told him that she had rights. That she didn't have to put up with him badgering her. But she was a different person than she'd been all those years ago. Therefore, all she did was pick up his card, turn around and hope that he'd leave really soon.

As Kent Olson watched Liana Mann slip his card into the side pocket of her polyester dress, he wondered when she would give in and call. And she would call; he was sure of that. She didn't like him being at her place of work; she'd made no secret about that.

He wondered why his presence here had bothered her so much. Was it because she had secrets she didn't want anyone here finding out about? Or had it been his bringing up Billy? She'd visibly tensed every time he'd said her husband's name. Or did her discomfort have more to do with his occupation? A lot of folks simply didn't like cops.

When he got back to the station, he was going to have to look again at the officers' reports from their visits with Liana. Not everyone was as kind to widows as they should be, and it seemed as if Grune and Evans had been especially callous.

Taking another sip of the surprisingly decent coffee, Kent reminded himself that there was another possibility—and that was that Liana didn't like him. Thinking back to how he'd acted, appearing out of nowhere, demanding that she talk even though she was in the middle of her workday, Kent realized Liana probably had a lot of reasons to want to avoid him. He'd been heavy-handed, cool and unsympathetic.

Again.

Those traits hadn't been the main reason for his being taken out of the detective pool and put into cold cases, but like his lieutenant had said, it hadn't helped.

After pulling out his wallet, he left enough money to pay for his breakfast and give Liana a decent tip. It wasn't a bribe, but maybe she wouldn't add *cheap* to his list of faults.

Back in his car he turned left, then carefully passed a horse and buggy. After pausing to admire a line of clothes fluttering in the spring breeze, he eased out on Highway 32 and headed west toward Anderson. Within twenty minutes the fields surrounding him gave way to retail stores and fast-food joints. Ten minutes after that he was back in the heart of the affluent suburb of Cincinnati. Pulling into a parking space at the station, he noticed that his dad's black Lincoln SUV was in its parking place near the entrance.

His father, Lieutenant Detective Richard Olson, was one of the most celebrated members of the police force. He was just one year from retirement, and now carried around cruise and resort brochures on Sunday afternoons. He and Kent's mom—who had just quit her own career in law—now spent hours dreaming about trips they were finally going to take and all the sleep they were finally going to get.

Kent was happy for them. He really was. Both of his parents had worked long hours and built successful, respected careers. They deserved to take as many vacations as they could—especially if it would give them some distance from him and the disappointment he'd just brought to the family name.

Striding toward the building, Kent focused once again on Liana Mann. She was brown-haired, blue-eyed, and had really pretty creamy skin. She looked as wholesome as the Amish women he'd spied walking with their children on the side of the road.

But unlike those Amish women, he was sure that Liana wasn't as innocent as she looked. He was sure that she knew more about her husband's death than she'd let on. He had to find a way to get her to talk to him. He knew there was more to Liana Mann than met the eye, and he intended to learn what she was hiding.

And he'd also recoup a little bit of the respect he'd lost…and hopefully get back into the detective pool and out of the basement's cold-case room.

As far as he was concerned, that couldn't happen fast enough.

Chapter Two

One week later

"Are you sure I can't convince you to appear at the show, Li? Not even for an hour?" Serena asked.

Serena's voice was as cultured and wheedling as Liana had ever heard it. But instead of making her nervous like it used to, now it only made her laugh. Serena Ketels owned Gallery One in downtown Cincinnati and was the reason Liana sold her large paintings for two and three thousand dollars each instead of two or three hundred.

Serena had given Liana financial stability...but that didn't mean the polished twenty-eight-year-old was going to get her to stand in the middle of the art gallery on display like one of her paintings.

"You know I don't want to put on a show. Even the thought of speaking to a bunch of your fancy clients makes me break out in a cold sweat."

"What if you only have to talk about your work? You don't have to stand around and sip wine or anything like that."

Like she'd ever done that in her life. "Serena, no offense, but you know I've never even been to a cocktail party before. I have no idea what to wear to one. And besides, what would I even say about my work, anyway? You know I don't have any training. I just paint."

"Liana, you are self-taught and gifted. You express your unique outlook on life through your mastery in oils and acrylics."

"Oh, brother." No, what she did was paint because it made her happy. End of story.

"No, listen." Serena started talking faster, the way she did when she had a plan and was anxious to put it into action. "I think you should talk about your feelings when you paint, Li. My clients would love hearing about that. I would love hearing about that."

Liana perched on her windowsill and chuckled. That statement was so *Serena*. The first time she'd met the gallery owner in person, she'd been flummoxed. Serena was everything Liana was not. She had dark hair, dark eyes and flawless skin and makeup. She wore designer clothes and heels the way other people wore old sweats and flip-flops. And she always spoke to Liana like she was someone special.

Since Liana absolutely knew she was not, she'd been sure that Serena Ketels was the fakest woman she'd ever met.

But later, when Serena had stopped by her house to pick up one of Liana's paintings, they'd started talking. Serena had confided that she was actually from a small town in Indiana and had worked two jobs to pay for her degree in art history. Minutes after that the gallery owner was soon wandering around Liana's art studio and talking about what a *genius* she was with color—and eventually declared that she was going to help Liana make a decent living painting.

Well, that had been what she'd heard. Serena had actually said that she knew people who would spend thousands of dollars for her paintings. Even the idea of such a thing was shocking.

Returning to the conversation at hand, Liana murmured, "Serena, I don't think when I paint. I…well, it just comes out from my heart to the canvas."

"Talking about *heart to canvas* is perfect."

Ah, no. No, it was not. "You know as well as I do that I never think about anything purposefully. Plus, I'm just a waitress in a small-town diner. Everyone's going to be disappointed." Or worse, they'd make her feel uneducated, unkempt and kind of worthless.

"I won't let them make you uncomfortable." Serena's voice rang with sincerity. "I promise I won't."

"You're a nice person, Serena. You really are. But believe me. I know what most people are like. They're still going to think I'm just a hick from a small town, which is what I am. And I'm fine with that. I really am—but that doesn't mean I want to stand there while strangers put me down."

"Liana, I think once people get to meet you, they're going to be willing to pay even more for your work," Serena replied in a quiet, firm voice.

"I don't know about that."

"I'm looking at *Sunset in October* right now. It's… it's so stark and bold and visceral. I think if you talked about why you titled it that, I could get over ten grand for it."

Liana almost spit out her coffee. "Are you serious?"

"Absolutely. You know I don't kid about money.

You're an up-and-coming phenomenon. And people are going to love that you're so modest and country. Please, won't you help me sell your work? I promise I won't make you regret it."

Everything she was saying sounded too good to be true—from the assured way Serena was speaking about people even showing up, to the care she was going to show Liana, to the insane amount of money she was talking about. It was the stuff dreams were made of.

But they weren't hers. "I appreciate everything you're saying. I really do," she added softly. "But I just can't do that right now."

The silence on the other end of the phone sounded like it lasted five full minutes, though it was likely barely thirty seconds. Still, it was long enough to make her palms sweat. "All right. I understand."

Feeling a bit like she won a battle but also curiously disappointed that she had, Liana thanked her before they at last hung up—just as a knock sounded at her door.

Foreboding filled her as she headed down the narrow hall to answer it. Sometimes Sol and Martha Yoder, her Amish neighbors, stopped by with a chicken or some vegetables to give her or even for a quick chat. But they were back-door friends.

No, the only people who knocked on her front door like that were cops. One glance through the peephole confirmed her guess. There was Kent Olson, standing straight and tall.

Invading her space.

She was irritated. What was he doing, just showing up at her house like this?

"Yes?" she asked the minute she opened it.

"I came to talk, Liana."

"We have nothing to talk about. Plus, you're here uninvited."

"I didn't have much choice since you never called me."

She refused to apologize for that. "I didn't even give you my address. You looked me up. Isn't that illegal or something?"

"Come on. You didn't think I couldn't find that on file?" His voice sounded almost reasonable. Not snarky at all.

"You should've called first."

He stuffed his hands in his jeans pockets, looking like he had all the time in the world to stand on her front stoop. "I couldn't risk you blowing me off."

She felt her cheeks heat because she would've done that. Pretty sure that he was checking out her blush, she mumbled, "This is hard for me."

"I know. But Liana, I told you this case was important. I didn't lie about needing your help."

"I might not be able to help you at all."

"We won't know if you won't let me ask you anything. Sorry, but I'm not going to give up, either. Now, are you going to ever let me in?"

She didn't want to. She didn't want to talk to him when she could be painting. Didn't want to talk about Billy. Didn't want to give this man even a moment of her time.

But it seemed Serena was right. Dreams don't often come true. Wishes rarely did, either. And then, too, was the nagging suspicion that God wanted her to at least deal with her memories of Billy. She didn't think it was a coincidence that this officer had suddenly appeared in her life. No, she had a feeling the Lord had brought them together so Liana would finally come to terms with all the memories that continued to surface from her marriage.

Maybe it was finally time to do His bidding?

Stepping backward, Liana motioned him forward. "Come on in. We might as well get this over with."

Chapter Three

Kent had been coaching himself about how to act around her all morning. He'd thought of topics that weren't likely to cause her to get her back up. He'd practiced ways of phrasing the things he'd come to say.

But none of that made a difference.

The moment he'd seen the way she'd been guarding herself against him, he was toast. It was time to finally start conducting himself the way he knew he should, the way his father would be proud of. It was the right thing to do, too. After all, he didn't want to make her life miserable. He just wanted answers.

After she closed the door, Liana turned to him. Her arms were crossed over her chest, and her expression was blank.

Kent realized he had about five minutes to change her mind about his being there before he lost even this bit of ground.

So he said the first thing that ran through his mind. "What are you painting?"

He'd surprised her. She ran a hand through her hair. Blinked. "What?"

Kent gestured to the front of the thin, baggy T-shirt she was wearing. "You ah, have some purple paint on you."

She looked down at herself. "It's magenta, not purple. And I'm painting a painting."

It wasn't much, but it was a start. "Will you show it to me?"

"Why?" Her eyes were filled with suspicion.

"Because I can't draw a stick figure." He gestured to the bare walls. "And… I don't see any paintings in here. How come?"

"I don't want to be surrounded by my own work."

As far as he could tell, Liana didn't want to be surrounded by much. There were three really fine-looking wooden chairs with ivory cushions on them. Next to each was a small table. There was no coffee table and only a sparsely filled bookshelf on a far wall. A bright rag rug covered the wooden floor. The faint scent of peppermint filled the air. The lights were off, making the room look cooler than it actually was. There was nothing on the walls. Nothing at all.

"It's peaceful in here," he said, surprising himself because he actually meant it.

She almost smiled. "Thank you. I like this room because it's so bare and plain."

"Where do you paint?"

"Down the hall."

"So?" He raised his eyebrows. "Will you let me see them?"

"Boy, you're not going to give up, are you?" Everything in her stance shouted that she had her guard up. He'd never been around an artist before but he had a feeling that she wasn't the only one to be protective of her work.

Ironically, her wariness made him feel protective of her. When he'd reviewed his notes, he'd surmised a lot of information that had been carefully phrased. It was obvious, to his eyes at least, that Liana had been put through the wringer by Detective Evans. She'd been considered a suspect for a brief time and had been subjected to some tough questioning.

The police had also searched her home and talked to her coworkers, her brother and even her Amish neighbors about Liana. More than once she'd dissolved into tears.

Officer Grune, in particular, had also made notes about the abuse Liana had received from her husband.

But even after the interrogation, and the waiting, and the uncertainty of having so many questions about her husband remain unanswered, Liana had carried on.

It was impressive. This pretty gal, so hurt by her brutal husband, was special. Suddenly, he didn't want to hurt her anymore—or at least not when it came to her inner sanctum.

"If you really don't want me to see your paintings, I won't make you," he said at last. "It doesn't have anything to do with the case… I'm just curious. I've never met an artist before."

"All right. Fine." She walked down the hall, leading him down the dark passageway. There weren't any pictures or artwork on the hall's walls, either. Just fresh white paint. He had the quick opportunity to spy a small bathroom, a bedroom with pink walls and a closed door before they disappeared into the last room.

And it was like walking into a different world.

Where the rest of the house was quiet and contained, this room had two tracks of lights overhead, no curtains on the four windows and an array of large paintings everywhere. The difference was almost blinding.

In the center of the room was a huge easel, a small table with a palette of paints on it and another table with water, paintbrushes, rags and a couple of pencils. The canvas on the easel had to be at least four feet wide and six feet tall.

In the middle of it was a wide swath of magenta.

"There it is," he murmured.

"There what is?"

He looked back at her. She was still in a defensive posture, and there was a bit of wariness in her eyes, too. And maybe curiosity?

He motioned to the splash of color staining her shirt. "The magenta." He grinned. "It stood out in your living room. I wanted to see where it came from." Of course, he'd meant something else, as well. Liana seemed cool, almost plain at first glance, but was carefully hiding a bravery.

After looking down at her shirt, she rolled her eyes. "Stained clothes come with the territory…but yes, I guess you found the magenta's source."

Honestly, Kent felt like he'd just found a whole lot more than that. This room was amazing and the paintings were so bold, it honestly seemed as if they were talking to him, almost illustrating her life.

It was a fanciful notion, but he kind of thought that Liana Mann seemed more like this room than the rest of her house. From the outside the place was pleasant but unremarkable. Once he'd come inside the doors, he'd been given some insight about her. The living room was pleasing and calming. Pretty because of its simplicity.

But now that he'd been allowed to experience this room—it was a revelation. It seemed to illustrate the fire that was hiding inside her. Explosive and bold. Practically daring someone to ignore it.

And the paintings? He'd never been one to appreciate abstract art like this but there was an element to the paintings that told a story. It affected him in a visceral way. At that moment, he realized that he'd seriously underestimated this woman. She wasn't just a victim of a loser husband. She wasn't just a country gal who worked at a diner and hid from the rest of the world.

She was so much more than that.

"I like them."

"Really?" Her eyes drifted over his face before she averted them again.

"Oh, yeah." He meant it, too. "They're different from anything else I've ever seen."

"Well, thank you."

She didn't seem to receive compliments easily. "Have you sold any?"

"Yes."

For the first time Kent thought he spied a hint of a smile on her lips. Intrigued, he motioned with his fingers. "Come on. Tell me more."

"Why?"

"Because I'm interested in your work."

"We both know you didn't come here to talk about my paintings, Officer Olson."

"My name is Kent. How about you call me that?"

"Fine."

Pleased to have made that bit of progress, he said,

"You're right, I didn't. But that doesn't mean I'm not being sincere. Now, tell me about your career, Liana."

"All right. I show most of my work at an art gallery in Cincinnati. They've been pretty popular." She edged to the doorway. "Now, can we go ahead and discuss whatever you came to talk to me about?"

"Of course." He gestured to the ladder-back chair next to him. "Want to sit down?"

"We can't talk here. Come on."

She led the way down the hall, out of the bright room and into the muted silence of the living room. He was disappointed; he couldn't deny it. A part of him felt like she was determined to keep that part of her personality safely away from him. Almost like she feared he would taint it.

When she chose the wooden rocker in the corner of the room, he wondered if she did that deliberately. All the other places to sit were at least three feet away from her.

He supposed he didn't blame her.

Forgoing the lumpy couch, he perched on the edge of a cushy-looking easy chair. "Liana, I'm going to be honest with you. Several months ago I messed up a case and got demoted. I've been assigned to cold cases and I need to solve several of them in order to get my old job back."

"That's why you decided to tackle Billy's case."

"It is, but it isn't the only reason. It's the department's obligation to close these cases. Our job is to serve the public and, consequently, Billy Mann."

She rocked back in her chair. "I'm sorry. Closing the case might help your career but it's not going to make much difference to mine."

"Why is that? You don't want the person who murdered him to pay for his crimes?"

"I want a lot of things, but that doesn't always mean I need them. Besides, to be real honest with you, Billy and me…well, we weren't exactly happy together."

"Libby said in her report that he was abusive. Is that true?"

"Yes."

"What did he do to you, Liana?" he asked softly. "I couldn't find any record of hospital visits."

She inhaled sharply. "Just because I didn't go to the hospital doesn't mean it didn't happen."

"You're right. Of course you're right. All I'm trying to do is get a better understanding. I promise."

She turned her head slightly away from him. "I don't want to talk about that time. It's taken me a while to get over the damage he did to me."

He was the son of a cop and a lawyer. He'd been on the force for years. He wasn't unaware of domestic abuse. He'd answered dozens of calls during his two years on patrol. But in spite of all that, he couldn't help but feel affected by Liana's words. It was like a punch to his gut. He could practically feel her hurt inside him, and it triggered a protective instinct in him that he hadn't realized he possessed. It didn't make sense and caught him off guard.

"How about we work together to find Billy's killer?"

Her face went slack. "Come again?"

"I intend to do my job, but I'm hoping there's a way I can do it without hurting you more. Perhaps, if you get involved, you can gain some closure."

"I don't know about that. I don't know if I need closure."

"How about this, then? Someone killed your husband. That can't be ignored or taken away. That means whoever did it has been spending the past ten years of his or her life free. Maybe even killing someone else. That's not right."

A second passed. Two. "No, it's not," she murmured.

"I'm going to need your help, Liana. You know the area, you knew Billy and you knew who he spent time with." He paused, watching that information sink in. Quietly, he added, "How do you think we can do this? How can we work together, Liana?"

"Are you serious?"

"Yeah." He was tempted to ask why she was so stunned but he kept his mouth shut. At least that was one thing he'd learned from his years on the force. If you stayed quiet long enough the other person would talk. Silence really bothered some people.

Looking more agitated, she got to her feet. "Officer Olson, I... I don't know what to think right now."

"About...?"

"About you. About going back to the past. About even trying to help you get the answers."

Boy, she'd been hurt. He didn't know if it was even possible to regain her trust in the police force. It was doubtful that she would ever think of him as anything but her enemy.

But he had to try.

"Maybe we can come up with a compromise," he said at last. "If I do my best not to get in your way, maybe you won't mind answering my questions."

"You're talking as if I have a choice."

"Everyone has a choice, Liana. God gave you a good brain and a heart. But here's what I can't ignore—Billy might have been a terrible person. He might have been a bad husband, and he might even have deserved to be punished for some of the things he did to you." He paused. "However, when he was twenty-four years old, Billy was abducted, half-strangled, shot and then thrown on the ground hard enough to create another fracture in his skull. Then his dead body was dumped in a place where no one found him for ten years. That's a real bad way to die."

She didn't say anything. Just stared. He wondered if it was from fear or because she simply wanted him out of her house.

Kent turned to face her and softened his voice. "Just as important to me, Billy never got the time to change. Maybe he wouldn't have. But Liana, sometimes people do change. They become better. They seek forgiveness and try their best to make amends. He never got that chance."

Something he said seemed to resonate with Liana. Her whole posture eased. "People do change, don't they?" Her voice was whisper-soft. "Some even become better."

"They do if they want to. If they're given the opportunity. All I can do is try to give him the chance he was denied. I can't save him, Liana. But I can make sure that the mystery surrounding his death is solved. I think he deserves that much."

"You're right." Looking resigned, she lifted her chin. "Billy wasn't good to me. But he wasn't all bad. At one time, when I married him, he was who I thought he'd be. So he…well, he deserves that much. At the very least."

Feeling relieved, Kent nodded. "All right, then."

It was only later, when he was driving home, that

he remembered the slight smile that had appeared on her lips. He also recalled the way that smile had affected him.

It didn't make sense. Not at all.

Chapter Four

Liana couldn't believe what she'd done. After just one brief hour in Kent Olson's company, she'd gone from actively trying to get him out of her house to agreeing to become his sidekick. What had she been thinking?

To make matters worse, she'd received an email from Kent first thing the next morning. In his message, he'd given her three dates to choose from—all within the next week. Liana was supposed to pick one today so he could work on their plans—which, she feared, was mainly to go see where Billy's body had been found. She didn't want to do that. She didn't want to go anywhere alone with Officer Kent Olson, and she especially didn't want to see the place Billy's body had lain forgotten for ten years.

But now it didn't look like she had a choice.

"Liana?"

The sound of her name shattered her musings and caused her heart rate to spike. Pressing a hand to her chest, Liana turned to Angel. "Sorry. I was daydreaming."

"You okay? You looked like you were gonna jump right out of those ugly shoes of yours."

Angel loved to tease her about her well-loved, scuffed Keds. Appreciating the break from her thoughts Liana smiled at her friend. "I'm good and my shoes are still on."

"In that case, care to join in the fun? We've got a full house, you know."

"Sorry." She picked up a water pitcher, refilled her customers' water glasses and took an order for pecan pie from an older couple.

But over the next three hours of her shift, she was jumpy and nervous. It was like all of her fears about Billy—and his murder—were haunting her in plain sight. Every time the Dig In Diner's door opened, she'd glance at it warily, practically expecting one of Billy's old friends to walk in with a loaded gun, or another cop in uniform to pull her outside for questioning.

"Liana, come on back to the office. We need to talk," Viv said moments after their last customer of the night walked out.

Viv didn't get irritated much, but Liana wasn't surprised at the woman's tone. Obviously, her boss had had enough of her mistakes. With a sinking feeling, she nodded. "It's my night to mop. I'll be there as soon as—"

"The mopping can wait." Waggling three of her long French-tipped manicured nails, Viv motioned her forward. "Come along now."

After glancing at Angel, who raised her eyebrows, Liana followed.

Both Viv and Gabe were sitting on the refurbished chairs in the back of their office, which was barely bigger than the average storage closet. Liana hesitated before sitting down on the third. Rubbing her palms along the seams of her blue polyester uniform, she sat as still as she could and waited for the reprimand.

What could she say, anyway? She'd been completely out of sorts today. Even the customers had noticed and showed their displeasure in their tips.

Gabe cleared his throat. "Liana, I'm just going to go ahead and cut to the chase. What is going on with you?"

"Nothing. I'm just having a bad day. I didn't sleep all that well last night and I guess it showed." Noticing that neither Viv's nor Gabe's expressions changed, Liana rushed on. "I'll be better tomorrow."

"Yeah, that's not really going to cut it," Viv said. "You're scared out of your wits about something. All day you've looked like you were about two minutes from running out the back door and going into hiding." She leveled a dark brown-eyed stare on her. "Why don't you give us all a break and share what's happened with you. And tell me the truth, now."

She knew Viv was right. Not only had she been acting strangely, but her bosses also deserved her honesty. "The truth is that I recently received some news that was kind of hard to hear," she admitted. "But don't worry. I can handle it."

Viv folded her arms across her chest. "How are you gonna do that, honey? By working through everything all by yourself?"

"Well, yes." It was what she did.

"Now, why is that?" Gabe asked.

The question caught her off guard. "I'm sorry?"

Gabe's burly shoulders lifted. "I thought you liked working here."

"I do."

"Viv and I try to take care of everyone like they're

our family. We thought you felt the same way. Am I wrong?"

"No." When Gabe raised his eyebrows, she added, "I mean, no, you're not wrong. You both are kind and I do feel like part of the family here." She took a fortifying breath. "But Gabe, I don't expect y'all to deal with my problems."

"What problems are those?" Viv asked. She had a gleam in her eye, telling Liana that she was pleased she'd caught her off guard.

It was obvious that Gabe and Viv were experts when it came to tag-teaming their employees. They were pros, and in comparison, she was a babe in the woods. "It has to do with the cop's visit here last week."

"How so?"

"He called me and then stopped by my house yesterday."

Gabe's expression turned into a hard mask. "Is he threatening you about something? You can tell him to go away, you know."

"Officer Olson hasn't been like that." She took a deep breath, starting to realize that the only person she was keeping her dark past a secret from was herself. "He's in charge of my ex-husband's cold case."

Viv blinked. "Say again?"

And that was how messed up her life was. Though lots of people knew that she was a widow, and some people had known that Billy had been in the running for worst husband ever, she'd never told anyone at the diner the real story. She'd gotten the job at Dig In two years after Billy disappeared.

"Billy, my husband, went missing ten years ago. I assumed he was dead. Seven months ago they found his body and examined it. And then they realized he'd been murdered."

"Liana, honey, you've worked here eight years. Eight! Why did you never tell us any of that?"

"I wanted to forget about it." Feeling Viv's hard-eyed stare burning a hole, she added, "And I was embarrassed."

"Because he died?"

Viv's voice was incredulous, and Liana didn't blame her one bit. She really should've tried to be more open about her past. "It wasn't because he died…it was because of who Billy was."

Gabe grunted. "Getting information out of you is like pulling teeth. Who was Billy?"

Frustrated, both with their questions and with her own reticence, she blurted, "He was a bad guy, okay?" Liana got to her feet. "For years I thought he'd just left me. But then, seven months ago, I found out that he hadn't just run off. He'd died. Now it looks like it was definitely murder."

Viv's eyes widened. "Oh my."

Liana swallowed. "Yesterday I agreed to help Officer Olson try to find the killer."

Viv snapped her fingers. "He asked and you agreed… just like that?"

Liana flinched. "No, not just like that. But it's not like I had a choice. He's a cop." Forcing herself to tell the truth, she added, "Plus, as bad as Billy was, he didn't deserve what happened to him."

"So you were just going to keep all this to yourself, come in here, take orders for eggs and then play detective on your nights off?" Viv asked.

Liana didn't appreciate the sarcasm. "Look, this conversation isn't easy for me. I… I'm used to hiding my bad parts."

"We all are, but sometimes we do such a poor job of hiding it, nothing is really hidden at all," Gabe said. "We care about you, girl. Let us help."

"Thanks, but there's not much you can do."

Gabe's voice deepened. "If you're afraid of us gossiping about your past, don't be. We wouldn't do that to you."

"I understand." Edging to the door, she said, "Is it okay if I mop those floors now? It's getting dark out."

Viv pursed her lips. "Sure, Li."

She walked out of the office feeling like her whole life was spiraling out of control.

And to see Angel looking more ticked off than she had all day—which was saying a lot. "Good. You're back."

"Sorry." She picked up the mop and ran to the back room to fill the bucket with hot, soapy water. "I'll finish up."

Angel reached for the ties of her apron, but then dropped her hands. "No, we'll finish up together. I've got a date, but I'm not going to enjoy myself if I know you're still here, toiling away."

"I'll be better tomorrow. I promise."

"I sure hope so." Throwing a hip out, Angel struck a pose. "I'm a good waitress, but even I can only do so much."

"Noted," Liana replied with a smile. Angel had been teasing, of course, but her attitude was as good a wake-up call as Kent's words about Billy's death and her bosses' reminders about their concern.

It was time to stop pretending that she was fine and

that she could handle all her problems by herself—especially since it was becoming pretty obvious that she was the only one who was getting fooled.

Chapter Five

On Sundays Kent went to church. It was as simple as that. At least, that was what his parents had taught him. Like a lot of his friends, getting up early on Sunday morning, showering, running to the car and then sitting on a pew for an hour wasn't something he'd looked forward to.

Actually, on a lot of Sundays, only a fear of his father yelling at him to *be respectful* had gotten him into the Lord's house.

But then, just when he'd started thinking that there were a dozen other things he'd rather be doing, the pastor would say something that sparked his interest. Then, next thing he knew, he'd be sitting a little taller, singing a little louder and feeling a little better.

Of course, Jessie Warner had a lot to do with his improved spirits, too. Jessie was in his youth group, loved being involved and often used her smiles to rope him in. And since he could think of nothing better than spending every spare minute with her, he'd had no problem being wherever she was.

Sitting beside his parents, Kent was thinking about

all of that as he watched the rest of the congregation approach the altar to take communion. Yes, coming to this same building for thirty years was a habit, but it was one of the best habits he had. The prayers and familiar rites felt like they were encrypted into his soul. He was better for it.

Did Liana have this in her life, too? If she didn't, was there a way he could try to encourage her to begin a journey of faith?

But of course, she would have to trust him in order to even consider taking his advice…and right now they didn't have that kind of a relationship.

Did they even have a relationship?

"Kent," his mother whispered. "Closing prayer."

Just in time, he flipped the page in his bulletin and got to his feet as the pastor offered them peace and forgiveness, then led them into the closing hymn.

Next to him, his father sang loud and proud. He'd grown up singing the same songs and now knew them all by heart. Kent and his mother shared a hymnal like they always did, sometimes smiling at each other when his father's perfect tenor soared to new heights. Yep, Richard Olson was a frustrated wannabe choir member.

Over and over the director had asked him to sing in the choir or be a cantor during one of the services but his dad had always refused, saying he was a cop, not a singer. But Kent knew better. His dad could handle being both just fine.

"You sang beautifully today, Richard," his mom said as the three of them made their way through the parking lot to their cars.

"Stop," he groused, though the faint red stain on his

cheeks betrayed his pleasure at the compliment. "You know I just like to sing."

"And I just like to listen to you. That's all." Turning to Kent, his mother smiled. "Want to join us for breakfast? We're going to Paulie's."

She asked every week. Sometimes he went but today his mind felt too muddled. The last thing he ever wanted to do was sound like an idiot when the conversation turned to work. It was hard enough being in his father's shadow without embarrassing himself in the process. "Thanks, Mom, but I'm going to take a pass."

"Other plans, son?" Dad asked.

"Just the usual—grocery shopping, laundry, cleaning."

His father studied him more closely. "Work going okay?"

"Yeah."

"Crier isn't giving you too much grief, is he?"

"Not any more than anyone else." He grinned at his father. Crier was the sergeant in charge of the cold-case division. There was a joke that the only time the sergeant ever smiled was when his grandchildren stopped by. Kent reckoned it might have some truth to it. The man could turn a rainbow into something to gripe about.

"That about sums it up," his father said. "Sergeant Crier's a good man, though. He listens, too. Don't forget that."

"I won't." He didn't doubt his father was right…but all the same, Kent knew he wouldn't be having any heart-to-hearts with the crusty sergeant any time in the near future. It had been hard enough to report to Crier after Kent's meeting with his lieutenant and being reassigned to the cold-case division. Kent hadn't been happy to be there, and Crier had made it plain that he didn't appreciate his territory being the dumping ground for cops who've messed up.

Before they discussed anything else about his new life in the basement of the station, Kent hugged his parents. "Enjoy your breakfast. Talk to you soon."

Five minutes later Kent was pulling out of the parking lot when he made a sudden decision to turn right onto the highway instead of left toward home. The Dig In Diner had a good breakfast and there was a chance it might be open. And if it was, he might even get to see Liana again.

Just the thought of that lifted his spirits.

Dig In Diner, like the rest of the little hamlet where it was located, was closed. It seemed the entire population took Sunday seriously. There were few cars on the streets—only an occasional black buggy meandered along the roads. Though he was tempted to drive by Liana's house on the off chance she might be outside, he refrained. Their relationship was tenuous at best, and he couldn't afford a single mistake to disrupt it.

Just as his stomach started to growl and he was regretting his decision not to head on home, he spied a blue house with Jay's Coffee painted in bright yellow letters on the sign out front. At least a dozen cars and trucks were parked in the lot, along with two bicycles. Eager to fill his stomach, he pulled off the road and took one of the last spots in the back, and then wandered in.

Jay's had embraced the blue jay theme. Glossy photographs of various types of birds and charcoal drawings of farms, trees and wildlife decorated all of the walls.

Other than that bit of kitsch, the shop looked as high-end as anything in his neighborhood did. The scents of fresh coffee and cinnamon and vanilla filled the air. The dozen or so tables were highly polished and sported curved paper placemats in various Easter-egg colors. The counter was freshly painted white and sported a chalkboard above with the daily specials. About half the tables were filled, and there were six or seven people in line. Two of them were Amish, but no one seemed to think anything of the twenty-something couple at all.

When it was his turn, Kent ordered an egg sandwich with bacon and fresh Gouda and a large latte.

Just after he paid, he spied Liana Mann in a corner. She was sitting by herself reading a book. A cinnamon roll and a large coffee were in front of her, each looking forgotten.

He knew he should leave her alone, but he honestly couldn't do that.

"Twenty?" the server called.

"That's me." He smiled his thanks as he picked up his drink and plate. Then, because he couldn't help himself, he walked over to Liana.

She glanced up when he approached. Apprehension filled her gaze for a moment before she smiled slightly. "Officer Olson. Hello. What brings you here?"

"Believe it or not, I was going to grab breakfast at the Dig In Diner but it's closed."

She nodded. "Pretty much everything is closed on Sundays around here except for Jay's."

Even though they'd ended things in a better place after his visit to her house, Kent knew he needed to tread carefully. They weren't friends, she didn't completely trust him and she was probably very much regretting her decision to help him out.

That meant he couldn't give her some line. He needed

to be honest. "I'm starving. Do you mind if I join you for a couple of minutes? Most of the tables are full."

After glancing around the room, most likely to confirm that what he said was true, Liana nodded. "I guess." She shook her head. "I mean, that's fine." With reluctance, she closed her book and slipped it inside her purse.

Kent figured he should feel bad that he was ruining her moment of peace, but he didn't. "Thanks," he said as he sat down. "I really didn't want to go eat in my car."

Her blue eyes almost softened. "I guess it's a blessing that you found me, then."

"Absolutely," he said with complete sincerity. "Liana, at the risk of sounding cheesy, I'd say this meeting was meant to be."

Meant to be? This guy. The more Liana got to know Kent Olson, the more she wasn't sure what to make of him.

Now here they were, sharing a cozy table and she had no idea what to talk to him about—especially because at the moment he didn't look anything like a cop. Actually, he looked like a normal guy. Well, as *normal* as an extremely fit, brown-eyed, blond-haired gorgeous guy could look in the middle of rural Adams County. He looked relaxed and at ease, sitting there eating his sandwich.

Liana took another small bite of the cinnamon roll on her plate and started hoping that Kent would be as good as his word and leave as soon as he finished.

After eating half of his sandwich in three bites, Kent put it down. "This sandwich is terrific. I can't believe I didn't know this place was here."

"Jay doesn't advertise. If you don't live in the area, I can't think how you would know about it."

"It's a great place. I'd take anyone here. Even my parents." He paused, looking mildly embarrassed. "Not that your diner isn't good, too."

"It's not my diner. I'm just a waitress there. That's all." She took another small bite of her treat. "And I know what you mean. I've got a few favorite spots that I would never take my friend Serena to." Latching on to his earlier comment, she said, "What did you mean about even your parents? I mean, if you don't mind my asking."

He shrugged. "I don't know what your parents are like but mine are pretty amazing."

"A lot of parents are." Though hers hadn't been in that category.

"You're right. I guess most people think of their parents as good people. Mine are that, for sure. But it's more…they're really good people. They go to church, volunteer for various charities and have both had successful careers. Plus, they've been married for decades. Most of the time I feel like I'll never be their equals, you know?"

She shrugged. Her parents were both gone, but when they'd been alive, they'd been carefully distant. Beyond encouraging her to marry Billy, they'd usually preferred to stay out of her life. When she'd been in high school, she'd kind of loved that neither of them were inclined to judge her actions or get too involved in her activities.

Looking back on those years and her tumultuous relationship with Billy, Liana had wished they had stepped in more. Their interference might have saved her a lot of hurt and grief.

Focusing on Kent's words, she murmured, "I'm sure your parents are proud of you."

He smiled. "Thanks, but you don't have to say that. I know I'm not your favorite person in the world right now."

His honesty made her chuckle. "You're right, you're not," she replied. "However, I might be starting to think that maybe you're not all bad just because you're a cop."

"Thank you, I think." Looking more contemplative, he added, "Just to let you know, we're not all bad. I promise you that." He looked down at his empty plate. "Huh. I didn't even realize that I already finished. I guess it's time I let you get back to your book. Thanks for letting me share your table."

Liana was starting to feel bad for not being friendlier, though she wasn't sure why. She didn't owe him anything. "You don't have to rush off, Officer Olson. You can finish your coffee."

He paused before getting to his feet. "Thanks, but a promise is a promise, right? I've eaten and now I'm going to leave you in peace…if you'll do one thing for me."

Her wariness returned. "What is that?"

"Will you call me Kent?" Before she could refuse, he added, "I mean, come on. It's not like I'm here on duty. We just happened to run into each other."

She might believe rain was in the forecast, but she was never going to believe that he just happened to be in her neck of the woods. But that said, she was starting to warm up to him. Maybe, just maybe…she could at least try to see him as something other than her enemy. "All right. I hope you have a good Sunday, Kent."

He grinned another one of his movie-star smiles. "It's

already been a pretty good one so far. Thanks for the conversation, Liana," he added as he picked his plate up and walked away.

She watched Kent take his plate to the counter, place a tip in the jar and then make his way outside. All without looking back at her.

She wasn't surprised. She didn't know him well, but already she was thinking that was how he did things. He walked through life confidently, gave things his full attention and then moved forward. Never looking back or second-guessing himself.

So different from how she lived. Sometimes she didn't think she could go five steps forward without retracing them.

Or maybe she was drawing him to be too simple. Just from their few conversations she'd learned that there was a whole lot more to him than she'd ever imagined. Little by little, he was starting to become far more than a nosy, promotion-driven cop. He was becoming someone far more interesting.

He might even be another danger…only this time to her heart.

Chapter Six

Adams Lake State Park was ninety-two square miles, had a number of hiking trails beyond the lake's perimeter and was someplace Liana had never been. Now, hiking by Kent's side, she was torn between admiring the scenery and the rare opportunity to be outside, and wishing she were anywhere else.

Kent, who was easily a good four steps in front of her, seemed to suddenly realize that she'd lagged behind. He glanced her way. "Sorry, I didn't realize I'd gotten so far ahead. I'll slow down."

"No. I'm fine. I was just looking around."

He glanced in the direction she was staring, toward a thicket of trees, some of which were flowering. "It's pretty, isn't it?"

"It is."

"Are you getting inspired for one of your paintings?"

She laughed, startled. "Ah, no. I was just thinking that it's been too long since I did something like this." Realizing that he was probably thinking she was referring to their main objective, she said, "I mean, be outside and enjoy nature. Not, you know…"

"Out looking for clues?"

She smiled at him. "Yes."

"I don't get out enough, either—especially not in May, when the weather is so good. I should, though. There aren't too many perfect days like today."

"You're right about that."

The weather in Cincinnati had four distinct seasons, and as far as Liana was concerned, only two of them were livable. Winter in southern Ohio was cold, damp and gray, with few opportunities to enjoy white, fluffy snow. Summer brought either bursts of torrential rain or humid, hot days. But spring and fall? Well, they were perfect. The days were mild and the evenings were cool. Spring brought acres of flowering trees. In the fall the leaves turned red and gold and cast a warm glow on practically every street. Though Liana had never lived anywhere else, she reckoned there were few better places.

Today, with the sunny skies and the temperature lingering in the upper seventies, was wonderful—and something not to take for granted.

There was a slight incline as they approached their destination. The trail had become a little more wild and rocky. Liana noticed a couple of beer cans nearby. "I guess even though we don't get out here much, some people do, huh?"

He frowned at the litter. "I should have thought to bring a bag to pick up debris. I usually do. Honestly, you wouldn't believe the number of kids who like coming out here at night. No matter how many trespassing signs are posted, they sneak onto the property and have themselves a good little party." Turning more serious, he added, "Every once in a while they think they're a little too invincible and build a campfire."

Remembering some of the places she'd gone with Billy when they'd been dating and she'd been far too naive, Liana kicked at a rock. "I guess this spot is as good a place as any if you're inclined to break the law."

"It is...if you don't mind getting caught and arrested," he said. "I never was over here on patrol, but I've gotten my fair share of folks at other area parks."

She liked that insight into his life. Though it was hard to think about him as anything other than a cop, she was now realizing that even in his work he wasn't necessarily the enemy. "What made you decide to be a cop?"

He looked surprised by the question. "I don't remember ever wanting to do anything else. My dad is a great cop. One of the best."

Remembering how much he admired his parents, she smiled at him. "I'm sure your kids will say the same thing about you one day."

He looked shocked that she'd said such a thing. "If I ever do have kids, I'm pretty sure they won't be saying anything like that. I'm never going to be as good a cop as my father."

"Come on. You're still young."

"Age has nothing to do with it. It's just how it is."

He closed off a bit, making her realize that she wasn't the only one with a secret. It was another revelation, which was humbling. She had developed a pretty good prejudice against cops over the past decade. Because of that, she'd begun to think of them as nothing more than self-centered people who had nothing better to do than make everyone else's life miserable. She'd been so wrong, it was embarrassing.

They walked a few more minutes in companionable silence. The only time they slowed was when they passed an Amish couple out for a stroll. The man sported a thick beard, signifying that he was married. Liana hoped their marriage was a happier one than hers had been.

"We found him right there," Kent said, his voice interrupting her thoughts—and transporting her right back to the awful reason they were there.

Scanning the change in scenery, she located the area where he was pointing. There was a slow incline, the ground giving way to limestone, followed by a series of jagged crevices. Shadows fell on them, cutting in at sharp angles, making them seem almost ominous.

Billy had lain in one of them for ten years.

It was dry out here. Desolate. She doubted even partying teens had ever hung out here—there were simply far too many other places that were less dangerous to be.

And so Billy had most likely just been out here in the elements all that time. She swallowed, imagining all the animals and bugs that would have discovered him first. Critters that survived on decomposing bodies. She shivered. Billy had likely not been much more than a skeleton with a couple of scraps of clothing by the time he'd been found.

The image rocked her. Why had she never really thought about all that before?

"Hey, you okay?"

"Yeah. I…" She turned to face him. "It just seems more real now, you know?"

His expression sober, he nodded. "I know. Are you up for getting a little closer or do you need a minute? It's okay if you do."

"I don't need a minute. I'm fine." Liana picked up her pace, anxious for some reason to show him that she was tough. Tough enough to not let a little thing like seeing the place where her husband's dead body had rested bother her.

Kent followed right behind, but she could practically feel the doubt and regret emanating from him.

She tried to ignore it. "So where was he?" No, he had a name. She cleared her throat. "I mean Billy. Where was Billy?"

He gestured to the right. "Here." When she pivoted on her heel, he held out a hand. "Easy, now. The ground is pretty uneven right here."

She took his hand, linking her fingers with his…and learned that it was needed. Oh, not for her footing. No, it was for the moment Kent knelt down at the edge and peered into the six-foot dip. "This is where Billy's body had been left, Liana. We found him here."

There was no choice. She had to do it. Kneeling next to him, she pressed a palm on the rock, felt its chalky texture graze her skin. Focused on what she could see instead of everything she imagined.

Peering closely, she realized nothing was there except for a scrape on one of the sides.

She pointed to it. "Is that mark from him?"

"Yeah. That's where the metal cuffs that were on his wrists scraped the rocks."

Billy had been cuffed. Even if he'd been alive when his body had been dumped, there would have been no way for him to have been able to escape. It would be near impossible without two free hands.

Billy hadn't ever been great. Eventually, he hadn't even been a good person. He'd regretted their marriage as much as she had and had taken out his frustrations with life on her.

He'd hurt her badly, both emotionally and physically. For the first couple of nights when he hadn't come home, she'd actually been glad. His absence had meant that she could breathe more easily.

But looking down at that fissure, seeing that bold scrape on the rock, Liana realized that Kent had been exactly right.

What had happened to Billy hadn't just been a sad event; it had been really bad. No one, not even Billy Mann, deserved to die the way he had.

Chapter Seven

"What do we do now?" Liana asked as they headed back to Kent's car.

Noticing that her voice seemed a little detached, Kent slowed his pace and studied her more closely. From the time he'd picked Liana up at her house to this moment, he'd been so impressed with her. Though there were so many roadblocks to their even having a friendship, she'd seemed to dodge them all with ease.

Instead of being sullen and wary, she'd asked him questions and been surprisingly forthcoming about her life. He'd even found himself thinking that she was so easy to hike with that maybe they could go to one of the state parks in northern Kentucky sometime in the future.

But then he'd reminded himself that this day hadn't been just part of a job for Liana. It was filling in gaps about her husband's death—perhaps gaps that she would have preferred to never know about.

Kent knew that confronting death was hard even in the best of circumstances—if those ever existed. However, coming face-to-face with a loved one's murder?

Well, that was another thing entirely…and even a decade's time couldn't camouflage the stark reality of that.

Glancing at her again, Kent noticed that while Liana appeared solemn, she didn't seem—at least not to him—to be on the verge of breaking down. He promised himself that he'd tread lightly to keep it that way.

"I might need your help again, especially if I deduce that there's a reason to take another look around your house and property."

"And until then?"

He tried to give her a reassuring look. "Until then, we don't do anything," he said at last. "It's all up to me."

But instead of looking relieved, Liana looked more interested. "Can you share what your next steps are?"

"Sure. Next, I'll need to go over all the dead ends and try to find something that everyone else overlooked."

She frowned. "Will that even be possible?"

"I don't know." He curved his hand around her elbow to help her around a gnarled tree root. "I mean, it's not like we didn't have good, dedicated officers on the case before." At her doubtful look, he tempered his words. "Hey, I know you feel differently."

"The officers questioned me like I had something to do with Billy's disappearance, Kent. It was awful."

"I'm sure it was." Slowly, he added, "I'm sorry to say that a lot of times the spouse does have something to do with a suspicious event like that."

"I didn't cuff Billy, hang him, drag him up here and leave him to…to…stay for a decade." Pure pain laced every word.

He winced, hating that he was the one responsible for this new wave of pain she was experiencing. "I realize that, Liana. Of course you didn't do any of that."

When she seemed to have collected herself again, he added, "Look. Cops aren't mind readers. All we can do is go on facts and experience and evidence. We might make mistakes but it's never intentional. At least, not in my experience."

"I know." She frowned. "Sorry. I wasn't talking about you."

No, just everyone he worked with. Kent understood her feelings, though. Just as much as he was aware that he'd made a mistake so big that a criminal got off. That was on him, and it would always be on his shoulders. "I'm sorry. I don't know what else to say."

"There's nothing you need to say." She exhaled. "I'm okay."

His footsteps slowed as he continued trying to get a read on her feelings. "Are you sure about that?"

Just as she was nodding, her eyes lit up. "Oh, look. Chipmunks!"

Struck by her sudden sweet tone, he stopped to look where she was pointing. Three little chipmunks, seemingly unaware of them standing there, were playing tag, their tiny white stripes making them look as adorable as Chip and Dale in a cartoon. He chuckled. "I'm guessing you're a fan of the little guys?"

"I am. Even though I know I shouldn't be, because they love to eat everything in my garden and make a big mess. But how can they not make you smile?"

"They are really cute." When one darted off, the two others chattered indignantly.

She laughed. "I could watch them for hours," she murmured before glancing his way with a guilty look. "Sorry. I bet you've got a dozen things to do." She stepped forward.

But there was no way he was going to make her leave just yet. Not when some color was returning to her cheeks and she was trying so hard to get control of herself. "No, Liana. It's okay. We can wait a minute or two. I've got time."

"Are you sure?"

"Absolutely." Honestly, some of the more hardened guys in the precinct would probably tell him to keep talking to Liana, to encourage her to let her guard down.

Maybe that was what he should do, but the two of them had already moved beyond that. He didn't want to be that jerk cop. Not with her, anyway.

When one of the chipmunks picked up a mulberry and stuffed it in its cheeks before darting off, Liana laughed out loud. "What a rascal!"

After they ran off a few seconds later, he walked by her side. "I'm glad we saw those little guys. Made my day."

"Mine, too." Sounding more tentative, she added, "You know, after everything I went through with Billy, I promised myself that I'd try to find joy as much as I could. It's not always possible, but I've found if I look hard enough, God gives us things to find every day."

"I don't do enough of that. But today's different, huh?"

"I hope so."

Feeling like she'd given him an opening, he said, "You don't have to answer this, but when you refer to what you went through with Billy, are you only talking about when he went missing?"

She chuckled again, but it sounded the opposite of when she saw the chipmunks. This time the tone was filled with bitterness. "Oh no." She paused. "Most of the time nowadays, I can't even understand why I married him. But I was a different person back then."

"How so?"

"Insecure. Alone. Mason, my older brother, and my parents were fine but distant." She swallowed. "I tried to be more independent, but that wasn't in my nature. I was a clingy child, I guess." Sounding wistful, she added, "I was constantly looking for someone to not mind me being near them all the time."

He hated that she thought her teenaged self should have been different. "Anyone would have been like that."

"Maybe." She shrugged. "I'm not making my parents sound too good, but they were. I mean, they were fine. There just was never a lot of money in the house, so bills were a constant worry. Then there was the fact that I was so different from my older brother."

"How so?"

"Mason was easygoing, independent, always happy— or at least happy enough." Liana darted a look his way. "I don't know what you did in high school, but Mason was a jock. He lettered in both football and basketball. Everyone loved him. They still do."

"What about you?"

"Me? Oh, I was just a year below him in school and had to deal with the ignominy of being the complete opposite of him."

"What? You didn't play quarterback?" he teased.

"Big surprise… I liked art."

"Obviously." He smiled. "You're really talented."

"I didn't know if I was or not. The art I liked wasn't really respected by my art teacher. She wanted my paintings to be on the traditional side. She favored details and precision. Her favorite students in the class created works that looked like photographs."

"While yours were different?"

Tucking her chin, she smiled. "Let's just say that she called one of my paintings a kindergartener's nightmare."

"Whoa! That wasn't very nice."

She shrugged it off. "My point is that I was kind of awkward in a number of ways, my brother was a star and my parents spent a lot of time stressed about money and the fact that they had next to no extra time. Ever. I tried to keep out of everyone's way."

"How did you meet Billy?"

"He was a year older than Mason and on his football team. He wasn't the star my brother was, but he was part of the same crowd." She shrugged. "After we graduated and it was obvious he was never going to go to college or even move to the city, he asked me out. Mason wasn't real thrilled about it, but by then he was dating Jeanie and working as a mechanic."

They had almost reached his car. "So you two started dating."

She nodded. "I was glad to finally be doing something right. For once I wasn't just the awkward girl trying to fit in. I was dating someone who'd been in the same crowd as my all-star brother. My parents were pleased about that. And, well, Billy seemed to really like me. He gave me a lot of attention, which I hadn't really ever had. And then we got married and the real world hit."

"Bills and chores?" Kent asked lightly.

"Yep. I found out pretty soon that Billy was good at

having fun with all the guys but not so good at holding down a job, paying bills or washing dishes."

"I bet that was hard."

"It was." She paused while they passed another couple, then added, "It wasn't all his fault, though. Like I said, I'd been more interested in painting or reading or just being in my own world. I wasn't all that good at cooking and I never made time to clean."

"Why? Because you were waitressing?"

"Oh no. I didn't start working at the diner until years after he went missing. Instead, to pay the bills, I did a lot of little jobs. I helped an older lady nearby with her house. Did some filing for a local business. A whole lot of things that took up a lot of time but didn't pay much. You see, Billy didn't want me working on the weekends or being around people he didn't know." When they stopped beside his car, Liana shrugged again. "Well, I suppose you can guess what happened after that."

The new, hesitant tone in her voice made his stomach clench, but he took care to stay impassive. As much as he wanted to hear about her past, he realized that Liana needed to talk about it, too. "I'd rather you tell me."

"I got tired and started complaining and Billy didn't care for that much."

"That's when he started hurting you."

"The first time he hit me, we were both so shocked, we just stared at each other. He apologized about a dozen times."

"But then?"

"But then I guess it didn't bother him so much." She wrapped her arms around her waist, like she was attempting to protect herself from the memories.

Kent got the feeling that she didn't want to finish her

story in the car. He leaned against the closed passenger door, wishing he could enfold her in his arms. But of course, he couldn't. He wasn't only afraid of spooking her; it was inappropriate, as well.

So he had to settle for words. "I'm so sorry, Liana."

"Me, too."

"I'm not judging…but was there no one you could reach out to to help you?"

"No. By the time I thought about getting help, Billy had started taking drugs and getting really mean. He was messing with his dealers, too. I mean, I was pretty sure he owed them a lot of money. There was no way I was going to get either my father or my brother involved."

"I'm sorry you were all alone. I hate that for you." Especially since he had a pretty good idea that both her father and brother would've dropped everything to help Liana.

She looked at him sadly. "Oh, Kent. There was no way I was going to drag them into my life…or make them pay the price for my mistakes." Before he could comment on that, she said, "Then one day Billy was just gone."

"Gone," he repeated.

"I figured he just got tired of coming home to me and took off with them." Looking at him, Liana added, "Please don't make me regret telling you all this."

"I asked you those questions because I wanted to get to know you, Liana. It wasn't a trick to get more information."

The relieved look she shot him was everything. Sweet and grateful and beautiful.

He smiled back as he held the passenger-side door

open for her. Kept that same expression as he walked around and got in on his side.

But once in the car, he was coming to terms with everything she'd said. Though he'd been honest when he'd stated that he had wanted to know her, he now knew one thing for certain—that Liana had carefully left out some details about what had happened between her and Billy. There was more to her story; he was sure of it.

Now all he had to do was figure out why she was still keeping secrets. Was she trying to protect herself, just like she'd always had to do?

Or was she now protecting someone else? Her parents? Her brother? A friend?

All Kent knew was that someone had gotten mad enough at Billy Mann to put a stop to whatever he was doing, and that someone was close enough to him to kill the man and then dump him somewhere he would stay carefully hidden for years.

Someone in Billy's circle knew how to do that. And even more important, they'd done it knowing that no one else in that circle would ever say a word about it.

Perhaps not even Liana.

Chapter Eight

Every time Liana thought that she had finally gotten Jeanie to start listening to her, she was proved wrong. It seemed today was no exception.

Jeanie also had a serious problem with the word *no*.

Liana was getting a really good reminder of her sister-in-law's habit of ignoring *no* during the last ten minutes of their phone conversation. Worse, Jeanie was pulling out all the stops. She was in full southern Kentucky mode—which meant that Jeanie was once again being as sweet as sugar while completely ignoring everything Liana was saying.

During the twelve years Jeanie had been married to her brother, Liana had had lots of practice with her sister-in-law's steamrolling ways. Most of the time she was amused. After all, it took a pretty strong woman to get the best of her headstrong brother.

However, today wasn't one of those days. She was just getting aggravated. She was going to hold firm, though. Sooner or later Jeanie was going to realize that she couldn't bulldoze Liana.

"Jeanie, I don't care what you say. I'm simply not going to meet your friend."

But just like the morning sun, she kept powering through. "Come on, Li. Don't say no. Wes is the nicest fella. He really is."

"No."

"Listen, I showed him your picture."

"You did what?"

"Honey, guess what he said? Wes said that he thought you were real pretty." Her voice brightened. "In fact, he called you *gorgeous*. You're gorgeous, Liana. What I'm trying to tell you is that he wants to meet you real bad. Why, he might even be smitten. It's as sweet as all get-out."

This was over-the-top, even for Jeanie. Then she put two and two together. "Wait. What picture are you even talking about?"

"Well…"

Liana groaned. "Please don't tell me you showed him the photo of me that you stuffed in the back of your wallet."

"Of course I did. That's where all of my pictures are."

"That picture is from two years ago."

"What's wrong with that? You looked real pretty."

"No, I look pretty different." Two years ago her paintings had started really selling well at Gallery One and she'd had more money in the bank than she'd ever had in her life.

She'd also been in a funk. Billy had still been missing, some people were whispering that he'd probably gone to another state and set up a new life, and a customer at the diner had called her *ma'am*. All that had forced her to take a long, hard look in the mirror. She hadn't liked what she'd seen.

Somehow, that long look had turned into a spur-of-the-moment shopping spree at a fancy department store over in Cincinnati, which had some kind of in-store photographer. Somehow, she'd agreed to let him take her picture after she'd put on one of her new outfits and spent an hour and two hundred dollars getting *refreshed* at the makeup counter.

The photos had been silly and fun. She'd laughingly texted a couple to Jeanie, who had been complimentary and sweet.

It was too bad Liana hadn't imagined that Jeanie wouldn't erase the photos, but would instead forward one on to Wes.

"You shouldn't have shared that picture of me."

"I don't see why not. You looked pretty."

"I looked pretty different." And not in a good way—she'd looked exactly like she'd been. A country girl in a fancy store trying to make herself into something she wasn't.

But her sister-in-law still wasn't getting the point. "Oh, who cares if you got older. You should still let me set y'all up. You can go out to lunch at Jay's Coffee. He's starting to serve sandwiches there now. They're real good, too."

"I know about the sandwiches." Kent had eaten one right across the table from her. "But no, thank you."

Jeanie's sigh sounded loud and full of despair. And then came the inevitable. "Liana, you aren't old. And all men aren't like Billy. You can find a man who will treat you better. I promise they're out there."

"I know."

"You might know, but I don't think you realize that you've got to try a bit."

"Oh, Jeanie."

"I'm serious, Li!" Her twang thickened like cold molasses. "Liana, honey, I'm sorry but no decent man is gonna just walk up to you at the diner or start knocking on your door. You've got to put yourself out there."

Oh, the irony. Kent had done both of those things. The first man in years who had made her even think of anything approaching romance was a man who had sought her out and knocked on her door.

Though, of course, Kent Olson wasn't trying to date her. No, he needed her help to solve a case and get a promotion.

"Jeanie, I appreciate what you're saying, but I'm not ready."

"Are you sure?"

"I'm positive. I promise I'll keep my eyes open and try to meet someone soon, but I don't want to be set up."

"What am I going to tell Wes?"

"How about the truth? How about you tell him that you're sorry but you spoke too soon and out of turn?"

Jeanie waited a few seconds to reply—and that wait made Liana grin. In addition to Jeanie's firecracker ways and bulldozer personality, her sister-in-law also had a good heart. "All right. Fine."

"Thank you."

"Do you want to come over soon? Mason would love to see you. He was just saying the other day that you haven't come over in a while."

That was the thing with her older brother. He wasn't the type to reach out to her. But she did know that if she showed up at their house for supper he would give her a big hug and be glad she was there. He wasn't really a man of words.

But for some reason she wasn't eager to see him. Maybe it was because of Kent's interest in Billy's death. Maybe it just drummed up too many memories that she'd thought were neatly locked away. Whatever the reason, for her sanity's sake, she needed to wait.

"Thanks, but I really can't right now. I'm pretty busy."

"We're going to be reduced to only seeing you at the diner, you know. I'm going to have to order a plate of eggs just to catch up on your life."

Since Jeanie didn't like eggs, that was saying a whole lot. "You don't need to do that. I'll see you soon. I've just got a lot going on."

"I hope you really do, Li. I'd hate to think you were hiding out like you used to do." She sighed. "Well, I guess I better go call up Wes and give him the bad news."

"For some reason I don't think he's going to be all that disappointed."

"You'll never know, though. Well, I'll call soon."

"I can't wait. Love you."

"Love you back."

She hung up then, feeling a little empty.

Which made her wonder if that was a good thing… or a sign that she was about to go down a very bad path one more time.

Looking around her house, she realized that the sudden silence was jarring. Usually, she found the quiet peaceful, but now all she felt was lonely. She should be still recovering from her afternoon at the state park with Kent.

She should still be rattled and shaken by those scrapes on the rock from Billy's handcuffs. But instead, she couldn't stop thinking about Kent and the way he'd been so sweet to her.

She should be regretting telling him so much about herself, for putting herself out in the open like that. But instead, all she could seem to think about was how right being with him felt.

Not a bit of it made sense. It didn't matter if he was a good listener or even if there was an attraction between the two of them that neither could deny.

All that mattered was that they didn't have a future. They were too different; she was too damaged…and if he ever found out what she'd been keeping from him?

It was likely he'd never forgive her.

She needed to remember that. If she'd learned anything it was that some things just couldn't be pushed aside and buried. Sooner or later they always came up again.

Chapter Nine

He'd decided to talk to his dad at his parents' house on Sunday instead of waiting until Monday at the station. Though he told himself it was so they could have more time, Kent knew that was a cop-out. The reality was that he was afraid to show too much weakness at work—which was laughable, since everyone there was very aware of all his flaws.

For most of his life Kent had idolized his father. With good reason, too. Richard Olson was a great police officer, a devout churchgoer and Samaritan and had been an even better father. Oh, Kent knew his dad wasn't perfect and that his father would be the first to point that out. But that knowledge didn't always register in Kent's weakest moments. During those times, the burden of attempting to live up to his father's reputation was always in the back of his mind and heavy on his heart.

That habit had cost him a lot. Since his demotion to the basement, Kent was trying to be better and to change. It was wrong of him to constantly compare himself to his dad. He was his own person and he needed to come to terms with both his strengths and his faults.

It was just too bad those changes had only happened after he'd lost a big case and almost lost his job.

All this was running through his head as he knocked on his parents' front door.

To his surprise, Dad answered. "Kent, why don't you use your key anymore?"

He took in his dad's appearance—faded loose Levi's, a white T-shirt that was untucked and bare feet. His father really loved walking around at home without shoes on. "Because I feel a little old to be doing that," he replied. "You know I have my own place now. Plus, you and Mom deserve your privacy."

He grinned. "Do we? I'll have to ask your mother about that," he joked as he waved Kent inside. "Come on in. I was glad you called to say you wanted to stop by. Your mother was so pleased, she's making a meatloaf and it's not even a special occasion."

His mother wasn't a great cook. She only made a handful of things well. But one of them was meatloaf. It was his favorite meal by far. Already looking forward to digging in, he glanced toward the kitchen. "Is she making mashed potatoes, too?"

"Of course. You can't have one without the other, right?" He closed the front door and headed toward the kitchen.

Kent didn't follow. "Hey, Dad? I want to say hi to Mom, but I came here to get some advice."

His father paused in midstep and turned to face him. "About what?"

"A case. A cold case." It was on the tip of his tongue to mention that other thing that was keeping him up at night. Mainly, that he was starting to have feelings for his main contact in the case. However, he decided to keep that to himself for a little while longer. Kent didn't need to guess what his father would say to that. Kent's fascination with Liana Mann wasn't professional in the slightest.

After studying him for a moment, his father ran a hand through his short blond hair that was now threaded with strands of gray. "Sure, Kent," he said at last. "I'll be happy to help if I can."

"Thanks."

"No need to thank me. We'll talk as long as you want. But first, you'd best come say hello to your mother."

When they entered the kitchen, Kent grinned at his mother. She, too, was dressed casually. But for her, that was a pair of tailored jeans, brown designer loafers and a crisp, light blue blouse neatly tucked into her jeans. But no matter how she looked, her smile was all mom.

"Kent, hearing from you this morning made my day. I was so glad I didn't have any plans. As soon as we hung up, I ran to the store to make a special dinner."

Giving her a hug, he murmured, "You didn't have to do that, Mom."

"I wanted to," she said as she kissed his cheek.

Spying the bowls on the countertop, Kent knew that his mom wasn't just making his favorite meal, but his favorite cake, too. "Did you make a Coca-Cola cake?"

"Of course." She beamed. "It even turned out well, too."

"Mom, you really didn't have to go to so much trouble."

"I know, but it felt good to make a big meal. Dad and I usually just have grilled chicken and vegetables during the week."

"Your mother is watching my blood pressure like a hawk," his father interjected.

"Good. We need you around." While his father playfully groaned, Kent lowered his voice. "Hey, Mom, I need to talk to Dad for a minute. Can we catch up during dinner?"

"All right." She glanced worriedly at his father.

"Work, babe," Dad said.

Her eyes narrowed, reminding Kent that his mother might be completely at home in her kitchen, but she was also a lawyer and no one pulled much over on her.

"It won't take long."

"Want something to drink?" Dad asked. "I think we have some Sprite somewhere around."

"Thanks, but I'm good."

"Come on into the den, then."

His father's den was in the back of the house. It was also everyone's favorite room. His father was a voracious reader and also collected signed editions of his favorite authors. Because of that, his den was actually a library. Bookshelves lined two of the walls—one of which was a good fifteen feet high.

Soon after they'd bought the house, Dad had hired a woodworker to build custom bookshelves that went almost to the top of the vaulted ceiling on one wall. Then, to make the crazy bookshelf complete, he had even commissioned an old-school library ladder to be built on rails for that one wall.

Kent couldn't think of a single friend when he was little who hadn't asked to climb it at least once or twice.

The rest of the room looked a lot like any other sixty-year-old man's private sanctuary. There was an old desk, file cabinets, shelves filled with old photographs and several plaques and accolades from a long career.

There were also a pair of worn leather chairs, a

scarred coffee table and a gas fireplace, which they sat down in front of. Just like they'd done for much of his life.

"Do you and Mom ever sit in here?"

"You know the answer to that, son. Your mother isn't one for being surrounded by all these books, leather, or all of my old junk."

"I guess not. She's always been more of a TV type of person."

Not looking disappointed by that in the slightest, his father nodded. "Yep. When you were little, she'd save five days' worth of soap operas to binge on Sunday nights. Now she's always got a new Netflix show to see."

"Did you ever mind that?"

"Mind what? That we have different interests?"

Thinking of himself and Liana, though he knew he shouldn't, Kent said, "You know, mind that you don't have more hobbies in common or something?"

He shrugged. "I never have. We both like being home, so I get to see her. Besides, I knew she was an independent woman when I married her, son. And, to be honest, after a long day at work, I kind of like my quiet time. She feels the same way." He kicked his bare feet on the table. "What's on your mind, Kent?"

"The Billy Mann cold case. Do you know of it?"

"A bit."

There was something in his father's tone that hinted that he knew more about it than maybe he was letting on. Diving in, Kent said, "I've gotten to know the victim's widow. Her name's Liana."

His father's gaze sharpened. "Is she cooperating?"

"She is. It took a minute, but we've agreed to help each other out."

"How so?"

"Liana is going to help me get a case solved and I'm going to help her move on." Well, that was his understanding. He certainly had never said those exact words to her.

"You must have done some fast talking to inspire that amount of trust."

"I don't think it's my fast talking as much as that we seem to get along for some reason." Realizing that he needed to give his dad more information, he added, "When I first met her, she was at her diner job. She'd hardly give me the time of day. But later, after I visited her house, and then when we had coffee at a little spot near work, everything changed."

"Hold on. Are you saying you went to this widow's house and asked her out?" Every word seemed to be laced with incredulity.

"Not exactly." After explaining how they'd run into each other on Sunday, he told him a bit about Liana's work. "You wouldn't believe these paintings of hers, Dad."

"They're good?"

"They're better than good. And like nothing I've ever seen. All full of color and blotches. None of it looks like it would make sense, but it does. And get this—Liana does all right with them."

"She's making a living?"

Kent nodded. "A gallery sells them for her. Most have sold for several thousand dollars."

He whistled low. "I'm impressed. It sounds like she's got a real God-given talent."

"Liana does. She didn't go to art school or anything. I get the sense that she paints from her heart."

"This woman sounds real special, Kent." He paused. "But listen to me. You're walking a tightrope. If you're not careful, everyone is going to say you shouldn't be working on the case at all. You don't want a conflict of interest," he warned.

"I hear you, but she's never been a suspect." He wasn't just saying words, either. Last year's idiocy had made a big impression on him. Big enough that he was done catering to his ego.

His father leaned back in his chair. "So is Liana who you wanted to talk about?"

"No. Dad, I think I discovered something." Briefly, he told his father about their visit to the park. Finally, he shared her news about Billy's drug problem and how he'd become violent with Liana. "Though a part of me wonders why none of this came to light before, I'm not going to dwell on it too much. After all, this is the opening in the case I've been looking for."

"It does sound promising," he said slowly.

"I want to talk to some of the guys who were Billy's dealers. Even though it was ten years ago, I'm hoping some of them are still around. Weren't you part of that drug task force around that time?"

"I was." He grimaced. "I put in two years on that force and thanked the good Lord the day I got out."

"I didn't realize it was that tough an assignment." He didn't say that lightly, either. All cops knew there were some units that were fundamentally different than others. But for a lot of them, they saw the bigger picture. It took everyone working together to make a difference.

"Some officers handle it real well. I didn't. I hated

it, if you want to know the truth. Give me a shooting or robbery any day of the week. Drug dealers are a whole other squirrel. Nothing's sacred. Some of them—well, I don't know if they're loyal to anything at all."

"The money, maybe."

His father shrugged. "Maybe, but I always had the feeling that some of the guys didn't seem all that influenced by money." He sighed. "Back then, when Billy Mann went missing, things were in a particularly bad way. Meth had just made the rounds and we had a real upswing in crime and drug overdoses. Though Detective Evans is good, back then we had about double the caseloads than we did time. A lot of things fell through the cracks."

Kent had heard from several veteran cops about those days. "It was a hard time, huh?"

"Worse than hard." Sounding weary, his dad added, "I was sure that a couple of them would lie about anything—and would sell their firstborn if it would give them an edge. That was what I found difficult. I could never understand the motivation, and because of that, I knew I wasn't the best fit for the job."

His father's frank opinions made his question even harder to ask. "Would you help me?" When his father flinched, he added, "Or, if you'd rather not, could you recommend someone I could reach out to?"

"Of course I'll help, Kent. I'd be glad to."

"Are you sure? I don't want to put you in a bind or anything."

"You won't. If one of those guys killed Billy and never had to face the consequences, I'd be more than happy to make sure justice prevailed. Besides, how Billy

Mann died and then was stashed away in the park wasn't right. No one should get away with such a thing."

"Thanks, Dad." He didn't even try to hide how relieved he felt.

"Don't thank me yet. I don't know if I can be much help after all this time." He paused. Kent could see him thinking hard. "Give me a couple of days to reach out to some guys," he said in a quiet voice. "I had a contact who I got along with okay. I did him a favor once. I doubt he's already forgotten that."

Kent looked at him curiously. "It must have been some favor."

"His wife was real sick. She needed to see a specialist and eventually had surgery. I called in a bunch of favors and made sure everyone treated her right. I would've done it for anyone, but he might see it as owing me. It's worth a try, right?"

Kent nodded. "Thanks again. I really appreciate it."

He shrugged off Kent's words once more. "You ready for dinner?"

"Always."

As they walked out of his den, his father placed a hand on his shoulder. "Just to warn you, your mother met a sweet young paralegal a couple of days ago. She's smitten with her."

Apprehension settled in. "How smitten?"

"Your mother knows that Danielle is single, twenty-four and likes to run."

"And let me guess… Mom is sure that Danielle and I would get along great?"

"Absolutely."

"Dad, I hope you haven't been encouraging her."

"I haven't, but we both know she doesn't need any

encouragement from me. Your mother might be getting older but she's still the same lady she's always been. She likes to meddle."

Kent grinned. He sure couldn't argue with that.

Chapter Ten

"I learned something new about you," Angel said to Liana with a smirk on Monday. "Girl, I had no idea you were so full of secrets."

They were cleaning up after a long night. Liana's feet hurt, her back ached and she'd gone from dreaming about eating one of Gabe's chicken fried steak suppers to simply longing for a hot bath and a cup of tea.

She was in no mood for one of Angel's guessing games...especially since it was about her. "I'm not up for your teasing tonight, Angel. I'm whipped."

"Sorry. I've got energy to spare."

Liana knew the girl was telling the truth. Her eyes were bright, she had a bounce to her step and all day she'd been wearing a chipper smile. "How come you're so peppy, anyway?"

"I have a date tonight."

"Oh boy." Liana glanced at Viv, who had been carefully refilling and wiping down salt and pepper shakers. Viv raised her eyebrows, which pretty much signified that she was thinking the same thing Liana was. That Angel picked the world's worst men to date. *Always.*

"Don't talk that way, Li," Angel retorted. "And don't think your silence means squat, Viv. I saw your expression and I know what it's supposed to mean. But this guy is different."

Viv shook her head in mock aggravation. "That's what you always say, dear. You're the queen of saying that the new guy you're seeing is different." She lowered her voice. "But they never are."

Liana kept her eyes averted and her mouth shut.

"I mean it. Sergio is dreamy and he has a job."

"That is impressive," Viv said.

Liana knew she wasn't being sarcastic, either. Some of the guys Angel saw seemed to make a good living off everyone in their perimeter.

"What does he do?"

"He works for the county." She paused. "He's a sanitation worker."

"Sanitation…wait, he's a garbage man?" Liana asked.

"He is." Angel lifted her chin. "Don't knock it, either," she said with a bit of fire in her voice. "It's an important profession. An essential one."

"I didn't say it wasn't," Liana replied. "Honestly, that's great that you found someone decent." Seeing that Angel looked like she needed a little pep talk, she added, "If everything works out with him, that would be fantastic. I'm really happy for you."

"Really?"

"Of course. You deserve to be happy. I hope he treats you like a princess…or at least is nice to you."

"He's been really nice. So far it's all great. I just hope it continues." Angel's shoulders slumped. "I just want someone who actually does what he says he's going to, you know? I'm so sick of being stood up or lied to."

She knew that experience too well. "You deserve better, for sure."

"We both do." She grinned. "But at least it's already happening for you."

"Why do you say that?"

"You know. Mr. tall, dark and detective."

"Officer Olson?"

"The one and only."

"Oh, please. We're not dating."

"If you aren't, you should be, and soon. We all saw how he's been looking at you."

What could she say to that? That he likely only wanted her because she could help him get out of the cold-case basement? That the only reason she was cooperating with him was because she needed to find some closure with Billy? "There's a lot going on between the two of us that you don't know about."

Angel eyed her with concern. "Do you want to share?"

"Not really."

Hating how hurt Angel looked—and at her own inability to open up about her past—Liana said, "Look, it's not personal. I mean, it doesn't have anything to do with you. It's about my past and my husband. Billy. I'd tell you more but I really don't like to talk about him."

"I know you weren't happy when y'all were married."

"You're right. I wasn't. But you know, I don't think he was, either. Our relationship wasn't the problem with him, but it sure didn't help." She frowned. It was the first time she'd ever actually thought about his feelings for her.

To her shame, Liana realized that over the past couple of years, she'd pigeon-holed her marriage into something that wasn't quite accurate. In her mind she'd been the good person who was always right and he'd been the bad person who was always wrong.

Yes, Billy had abused her and treated her terribly. But now, looking back on those days, she could honestly say that she wished she hadn't lied to so many people about what was happening. Over and over different people in her life had encouraged her to speak about her bruises. More than one person had promised to help her move someplace safe. But she'd been so ashamed that she'd rebuffed their offers of help.

Now, though, she realized they'd needed each other's weaknesses in order for their marriage to thrive. Or... perhaps it was the other way around. Their combined faults allowed their relationship to disintegrate.

Returning to the present, Liana said, "Kent, I mean Officer Olson, is probably not my prince charming, but I don't really need one. At least not anymore."

Viv walked over. "I should say not, now that you're a famous artist and all."

She was so shocked, she couldn't even think of a word to say. She merely gaped at them both.

Angel giggled. "Come on. You didn't think you were going to keep your other life a secret, did you?"

"I wasn't keeping it a secret."

Viv popped a hip out and placed a hand on it. "No? You were just...what? Thinking we wouldn't be happy for you?"

"I don't know. I started painting as my release. As a way I could express myself when I was so frustrated when Billy went missing and the cops kept questioning me and I didn't have the answers they wanted."

She paused, trying to convey how confused she'd

been but also how used to keeping everything she was thinking deep inside her, like a locked vault.

"I never thought anything would come of it. But then one day I realized I had like twenty paintings propped all over the walls of my house and I didn't know what I was going to do with them. So I decided to put them on eBay."

"Let me guess. They sold in a heartbeat," Viv said.

"No, but they did sell pretty fast." Though she was a little embarrassed to tell her story, feeling like it was close to bragging, it still felt good to talk about the experience. "I couldn't believe it."

"What did you do with all your money?" Angel asked.

"I didn't make that much. I honestly hadn't thought anyone would want them so I hadn't put up much of a price. But to answer your question, I went out and bought some more canvases and paint." Smiling at the memory, she added, "Then I painted some more."

"You're practically a celebrity," Viv teased. "I had no idea you were so famous."

"I'm not. But a gallery owner bought some of my paintings, and when she offered to pick them up from me I agreed because I didn't want to pay the shipping, and we started talking. Next thing I knew, she was buying even more and selling them in her gallery for a whole lot more than I ever imagined."

Angel nodded. "And the rest is history."

Liana shrugged. "I guess it is."

"None of us had any idea about it, either," Viv said.

"Maybe that's good," Angel added. "I mean, I would've told someone."

"Or ten someones." Viv winked.

Wanting them both to see that she hadn't meant to exclude them from her life, that it had gotten bigger than she'd ever imagined, she added, "I wasn't keeping this a secret from you two on purpose. I just…well, I guess painting is a part of me that I don't know how to share." Realizing that didn't exactly convey what she meant, she groaned. "Sorry, that still didn't sound too good."

"You don't need to explain it any more. I get it," Viv said. "You didn't talk it up because this painting of yours is special to you. It means something," Viv said.

"Yes." She couldn't have described it any better. It really did mean something to her. She was vulnerable where it was concerned. "I don't expect everyone to like what I paint, but I'm not really good at criticism." She shrugged. "I don't know why." Something occurred to her then. "How did you find out about it?"

"I saw the ad in *Cincinnati Magazine* when I was waiting at the dentist."

"It had my name?"

"It did. And a hazy picture of you." She frowned. "You looked a little odd—almost like you had a pile of makeup on your face. But it was you, all right."

"That picture has been the bane of my existence. I didn't know Serena put it in a magazine." She frowned. "I wish she would've told me she was going to put my picture out."

"I'm glad she didn't ask your permission," Angel said. "If she had, you would've said no and then we'd still be talking about you and wondering what you did on your days off."

Liana figured she should probably be irritated at them gossiping about her, but she couldn't really blame them. It was normal to talk about people one spent forty hours a week with. "Well, now you know."

"Gabe and I were saying that we might go to that fancy-pants gallery and get our picture taken with you and one of your paintings. We're free on June eighth."

"June eighth?"

"Uh, yeah. That's the night of your big show, Liana."

"Oh. Well, don't go to the gallery. I mean, don't go if you want to see me there, I mean."

"Because?"

"Because I'm not going."

Viv frowned. "Why not?"

"I never go to the shows."

"How come?" Angel pressed.

"I don't belong in that world. People are going to want me to talk about my work and I'm not going to be able to say much other than I liked painting the canvases. It would be awful."

"Maybe it won't be like that," Viv said. "You won't know if you don't try."

Feeling awkward, Liana said, "I appreciate your words, but the problem is that I don't think I'm ready to try. Not yet, anyway." Hating the way her friends looked so disappointed, she added, "But y'all are welcome to come to my house and see the paintings there anytime. I mean, if you want."

"I want," Viv said.

"Me, too," Angel said. She clapped her hands together. "We'll have a party or something."

"You two are too much." She knew she was blushing, but she was really gratified. They'd made her feel good. Proud, almost.

"Anytime you want, come over, though you might

want to call or text me first. I don't always hear the doorbell."

"It's going to be soon, chickadee," Viv said. "I can't wait to see your work."

"Viv, I want out of here!" Gabe called out. "We've been going strong since five this morning. Stop chatting!"

"I think Gabe's had enough for one day," Viv said with a chuckle. Looking around the dining area, Viv added, "Things around here look good enough. Anything we missed can be fixed in the morning. Let's go home, girls. We've got things to do."

"That's right," Angel added. "I've got a hot date with a garbage man and you, Liana...well, you've got your paintings."

Liana chuckled. "I sure do." But right at that moment she wasn't looking forward to them at all. Instead, she was wishing she had someone waiting to see her, too. Coming home to an empty house wasn't all that comforting.

Maybe it never had been.

As she started her car thirty minutes later, Liana realized Angel was right. They both deserved good relationships.

One day, she hoped she would actually have one.

Chapter Eleven

"It's hard to believe we've never gone on calls together," Kent's dad said. "Don't know why."

He did. All his life, Kent had known his father was one of the best cops in the police department. Men and women in the department had told him so during barbecues, picnics and even the occasional funeral. No matter what the occasion, one or two officers would take the time to tell him how amazing his father was.

And that had been nothing compared to the things he'd heard about his dad at the academy. More than one instructor had told him that he would never measure up.

Kent had been proud of his father. So proud. But his father's reputation had been daunting. Following in those footsteps hadn't just been hard, it had felt like he was swimming in them. Over time, instead of becoming more humble, he'd developed a persona to combat almost any naysayer. He'd thought it would cover up his lack of experience, make his fellow officers take less notice of his mistakes. But the only person he'd been fooling had been himself.

"I know why," he finally said as he took the exit off 32

and headed east. "I was trying so hard to prove myself, I forgot that I still had a lot to learn."

"I know you think you should've done something differently, but I think you need to give yourself a break. The past is in the past. Accept it, make peace with it and move on."

"If I hadn't been so full of myself, I could've made a lot less mistakes."

His father chuckled softly. "So you wish."

"What's that supposed to mean?" He was feeling mildly irritated. Here he was, trying to be completely honest about his faults, and his dad looked like he was about to burst out laughing.

"It means that everyone makes mistakes, Kent. Everyone comes to this job with chips on their shoulders about something. And by the time they're my age, they have regrets about all sorts of things." He grunted. "Lots of things."

"Even you?"

"Especially me." He grinned at his son. "I didn't get so awesome overnight, you know."

"I'll keep that in mind."

"I hope you will." Sobering, Dad added, "Now that I'm close to retirement, I have the luxury of being able to look back. I've learned some things."

"Such as?"

"Such as God doesn't make mistakes."

That was the last thing Kent expected him to say. His father was a faithful man; he knew that without a doubt. But he'd never heard him say something like that in the middle of a workday. "I know God doesn't make mistakes, but we're talking about plain old men and women, right?"

"No, we're talking about regular folks doing stupid stuff and learning from their mistakes. The Lord gives us those opportunities, Kent. He puts obstacles in our life to stumble over or trip on so we don't stumble and trip for the rest of our lives."

"I know I won't ever turn in evidence without double-checking everything again."

"Every person in the department has their issue. I promise you that. Even Crier."

He decided not to comment on that. Sergeant Crier was Kent's boss now in cold case world. Everyone in the precinct gave him a wide berth, since he seemed to always be in a grumpy mood. Kent respected him—no one who knew about Sergeant Crier's success in closing cold cases wouldn't respect him. But even so, Kent was looking forward to the day when he wasn't sharing a room with him in the basement.

Looking out the window at the houses that were starting to appear—each one more run-down and out of hope than the next—he frowned. "This looks familiar.

"I heard two of the men you used to deal with have set up shop around here."

"We'll see if anyone is around. It might take a while."

"I know." Kent pulled into a parking lot of a youth center next to a run-down park. Two women with toddlers were next to the playground. A group of teenagers played basketball on a court on the other side.

When he and his father got out of the 4Runner, one of the boys looked over at them and scowled. He muttered and nudged one of his buddies. Kent noticed then that one of the players was older and seemed to be in charge. After he said something to them all, the teens started playing ball again.

It was evident that his father had noticed the interaction, as well. Looking pleased, he said to Kent, "Let's go have a chat." Then he set off toward the teenagers. Kent picked up his pace and stayed by his side.

Though neither of them were in uniform, of course, Kent figured they might as well have *Police* emblazoned in bright orange letters across their chests. The closer they got, the less the boys were making any effort to even pretend to be playing ball.

Practically every eye in the area was focused on them.

The back of Kent's neck started to tingle. For the first time since he'd joined the force, he was worried about the safety of his partner. Not that he didn't think his father could handle himself, but Kent doubted he could shield him sufficiently if anyone pulled out a gun.

"You want to take the lead or me?" his father asked.

"I'm going to let you, since you've worked with some of these guys—or guys like them."

"One or two of them are here. Maybe not standing in the park but they're around. I'm sure of it." On the heels of that statement, he walked forward to the boys on the court, each one blatantly staring at them. "Who's winning?"

"Who wants to know?" the teen who'd first glared at them said. Right away, though, it was obvious that the guy wasn't a teenager at all. Kent guessed he was closer to twenty-four or twenty-five.

Just as Kent was about to play it casual—or as casual as possible, given that they were obviously cops—his dad charged forward.

"I do, Joe. Remember me?"

Suspicion filled the guy's eyes. "Nobody calls me Joe anymore."

"Do you want me to call you something else?" Richard asked easily.

"I don't want you to call me anything." Lifting his chin, he added, "What are you doing here, Olson?"

"I need some information."

"I didn't do anything."

Kent spoke up. "It's about something that happened ten years ago."

Joe—or whatever his name was—looked shocked. Kent figured he had good reason to be. He was pretty shocked himself about the way the conversation was going.

"Ten years was a long time ago."

"It was," his dad murmured. "You were into some bad stuff and I was thinner."

To Kent's amazement, Joe chuckled. "You had blonder hair, too…and a whole lot more of it."

Seeing that the other guys were shifting restlessly and starting to get uneasy, Kent said, "Nobody's in trouble. All we need is some information about a cold case. Then we'll be on our way."

Still staring intently at his father, Joe said, "As much as I appreciate what you did for me back in the day, I don't see why I should do a thing to help you now, Olson. Like we said, a lot of time has passed."

"I'm asking because it's about Billy Mann." His dad waited a beat, then said mildly, "Remember him?"

Joe's eyes flared before they went blank again. "What about him?" he asked as he took a step back, like he was trying to get some space from Billy's memory.

"His body was found a couple of months back," Kent

said. "He'd been killed and left out near Adams Lake Park." He pointed toward the hills. "He rotted there for ten years."

Distaste—or maybe it was dismay—filled Joe's expression before he tamped it down tight again. "Like I said, ten years is a long time. Billy Mann ain't my problem."

"We know he was using and dealing a little."

Joe rolled his eyes. "He weren't much of a dealer. He weren't much of anything."

"We're trying to find out who killed him," his dad said.

"So you think it was me?"

"Was it?" Kent asked.

"Of course not." He scoffed. "Billy Mann wasn't worth my time."

"I wouldn't have come out here if I didn't need information, Joe," his dad said. "I agree that Billy wasn't much to speak of, but my job is to solve murders, not judge victims."

Joe looked at them both for a long moment, then motioned for his buddies to move away. The guys looked irritated but did as he asked. Two minutes later only the three of them were standing on the court. "Look," Joe said. "I get that you have to do your job, but that guy has nothing to do with me. Not who I was back then and not who I am now."

"I get that. And I get that you're not anxious to revisit your past. But Billy's widow needs some closure." His father lowered his voice. "I heard you've got a wife and kids of your own now. Surely, you can relate to her worrying."

Joe scoffed. "I don't know if you two are telling me crap or if you think I'll believe anything you spout off."

His dad looked confused. "Tell me why you'd say that."

"Everyone knew Billy Mann beat her all the time. And when he wasn't doing that, he did a whole lot of stuff that was just plain wrong."

"Such as?" Kent asked.

Joe eyed Kent with disdain. "Like not giving her any money for food and laughing about it. I can't figure out why you'd think I'd buy that she'd spare him a second thought. If I was her, I'd be dancing on his grave."

He hated the thought of Liana going hungry. It physically hurt him. "I knew he abused her," Kent said, struggling to keep emotion out of his voice. "I didn't know everyone knew it."

"Of course everyone knew. It wasn't a secret." Joe shook his head. "I remember I saw her once, her face all swollen and black-and-blue. She was skinny as a rail, too." He paused, then added, "One of my guys was worried about her. Like, enough to think that she needed to go to the hospital."

Kent was blown away, hearing this former gang member talk about seeing Liana like that. It also made her situation seem more real. It wasn't that he hadn't believed her; it was just that he hadn't completely put the woman he knew now into that role.

His father looked Joe in the eye. "I saw her from a distance once. She was a timid thing. She never filed charges against Billy. Never went to the hospital, either. I would've helped her if I could, but our hands were tied."

Joe shrugged. "I told my guys if someone was beating my sister or my daughter like that, I'd take the law into my own hands." He paused long enough to look them both in the eye. "You two might think differently, but I'm telling you this. Sometimes you gotta do what's right, even if the rest of the world says it's wrong."

Thinking about Liana, about just how much Billy had hurt her, about the way she was skittish over everything even after all this time… Kent knew that what Joe was saying wasn't exactly wrong.

But then, just as they were pulling into the police department parking lot, something Joe said struck a chord with him. *If someone was beating my daughter or sister…sometimes you gotta do what's right.*

Suddenly, Kent wondered if he'd been going about the case all wrong.

Chapter Twelve

Liana wasn't sure why she'd said yes, but she supposed she was a glutton for punishment. Why else would she have agreed to a dinner date with Kent?

It had all happened so quickly, too. One minute she'd been sitting on the couch, flipping through old episodes of *Top Chef,* and the next she was holding her cell phone, wondering what in the world she'd just done.

Actually, she'd been at a loss for words while he'd told her that he really wanted to take her out to spend time with her. Not to ask her another twenty questions about the man she tried so hard to forget.

When she'd finally gotten her voice back, she hadn't been all that sweet. Actually, she'd kept telling him that he didn't need to buy her a meal to get help for his case. That was a sure thing.

He'd had the nerve to sound offended. And maybe hurt, too.

Which, in the end, was what had made her say yes. Kent might have originally reached out to her because of the case, but she was enough of a realist to know that his invitation wasn't because of any misplaced guilt or lies. Cops didn't offer dinner invitations as part of their job. Moreover, an upstanding man like Kent could no doubt ask out any woman he wanted. He was not only extremely good-looking, he had a good job, as well. He also obviously came from a cushy family with lots of support.

There was only one reason he'd asked her out, and that was because he wanted to. And when he told her that, with no attempt to temper his words, Liana had melted.

He had just given her everything she'd ever wanted—honest words and real emotion. Not lies. Not slick smiles covering years of manipulation. She wanted to feel something real.

He'd given that to her.

Now here she was, dressed in a dark ruby-red maxi dress that she would have never bought on her own but had been coerced to by Angel and her online shopping expertise.

Looking at her reflection in the mirror, she studied herself this way and that. She usually didn't wear bold colors or prints. But the ruby shade brought out the color of her lips and the flush of her cheeks. It even drew attention to her blue eyes, something she'd never considered highlighting before.

She'd added some flat sandals with gold braiding around the toes and a pair of gold hoops that Serena had given her after her first big art show.

None of this was her. But she couldn't deny that even with her hair up in a carefully arranged messy ponytail, she looked pretty good.

When her doorbell rang, she picked up her small purse and opened the door to Kent. "Hi."

"Hey, Liana." He smiled at her. "You look gorgeous."

She smoothed her hands down her thighs. "Hardly that."

Still gazing at her, he shook his head. "No, definitely that. I'm sorry for staring. I guess it's, ah, the way you have your hair done. It caught me off guard." He flashed a smile. "Are you ready?"

"I am." Pulling her keys out of her purse, she said, "I'll just lock the door and we can go."

He pressed a hand on hers. "Hold on. Turn on a light inside. And one by the front door."

Obediently, she flicked the switches. "Why?"

"It's not safe to leave the house dark."

"It's fine. I do it all the time."

"I'm going to lose my mind if I know you're walking into a dark house whenever you work late at the diner. Help me out and don't do it again. Okay?"

She'd come a long way from the days when she was Billy's wife. Back then he'd used whatever method he could to make sure she followed every directive. Within the first months of their marriage, she'd learned to simply do as he wished in order to keep the peace—and her sanity.

When he'd gone missing, she'd vowed to never become a victim again. Or, at the very least, to never simply agree with a man's wishes in order to make him happy.

So it wasn't easy to simply let him have his way or to say yes without arguing. But reason reminded her that he wasn't trying to control her; he was trying to keep her safe.

"Okay," she said at last.

He chuckled under his breath as he opened the passenger-side door of his SUV. "Boy, for a moment there I was afraid you were going to make me start spouting facts and figures to prove the need for lights."

"I'm not that stubborn," she said as she buckled her seat belt after he joined her in the car.

"Liana, you're one of the most stubborn women I've ever met."

"Then you may count yourself as blessed indeed. I promise there's a whole lot of women who are far more stubborn than me. Besides," she added, "I happen to think I'm just independent."

"I think I'll agree with you on that one." He shifted gears as he sped down the road. "You're impressive. That's what you are."

"Where are we going, by the way?"

"There's a good seafood place on the Ohio River," Kent said as he headed south on the interstate. "Ernie's. Have you ever been there?"

"I've never even heard of it."

"Oh? Well, you're sure to be happily surprised." Smiling big, he added, "You should see the king crab feast they serve up. They fly in the crab a couple of times a week, and serve it with drawn butter, lemons, dirty rice and grilled vegetables to die for. I promise you're going to love it."

"I bet I would…if I wasn't allergic to crab."

The crestfallen expression that lit his face was picture-worthy. "Oh my gosh, Liana. I'm such a dope. I didn't even think to ask." He drummed his fingers on the steering wheel. "We could go all the way down to Newport. There's a lot of restaurants to choose from there."

He was speaking of Newport, Kentucky, the first town just on the other side of the Ohio River from Cincinnati. It was nice there, with the revitalized shopping area that offered a wide array of dining and bar options.

"I like Newport, but I'm going to like Ernie's, too."

"I don't want to take you someplace where you can't eat."

"I can eat fish, just no crab or shrimp." Feeling bad now, she said, "I'm sorry. It was so much fun to tease you, I hadn't really thought of how rude that was."

"No, this is on me. I know better than to spring this place on a date."

"I promise I still want to go."

"All right," he said as he got in the right lane. "It's the next exit. Let's take a peek. If you don't like it, we'll go."

She decided right then and there that no matter how bad the fish was, she was going to eat it and not say a word. "Sounds like you've been going here a while?"

"Ever since I was little. Ernie's was my dad's favorite place. It still is. So every Father's Day we would go. And his birthday."

"That's nice. I like that y'all have so many traditions."

He glanced her way again. "You don't talk about your parents much. Did you grow up going to favorite places, too?"

"Not really. My mom was a pretty good cook." Realizing she was making her mother sound like a chef, Liana clarified her words. "I mean, Mom could take pretty much any five things in her pantry, add some salt, lard, ingenuity and produce something tasty."

Liana shifted in her seat, wanting to watch her words, to try to describe life with Mason and her parents without sounding pitiful or bringing up a bunch of stereotypes. "We didn't have a lot of extra money for going out, which meant that even dinners at the diner where I'm working were a big deal. The worst thing for my mom was to go out and realize she was paying good money for food that wasn't half as good as she could produce." That was true, too. It was also a much better depiction than how things usually were, which was that her parents weren't around much and Mason, the football star, always had first dibs on what was in the pantry.

"You were fortunate. My mom is terrific but can only make about a dozen things. She rotates them like clockwork."

"It might sound odd, but that makes me happy."

"Why is that?"

She shrugged her shoulder, wanting to be completely honest but not wanting to sound insecure or even snippy. "I guess it makes me feel good to know that the two of us aren't really that different." Realizing how that sounded, Liana tried to rephrase it. "I guess sometimes, when I look at our situations, I feel like you have all the advantages. You said your mom was a lawyer and your father had a good job, that he's some kind of superhero cop."

"I thought you got along with your parents?"

"I did. I mean, I did well enough. It's just that, well, college wasn't ever in our conversations and I wasn't ever really close to them, though Mason and I are now."

"You're selling yourself short. You've been through some really difficult times yet you haven't let it get you down. Now you're painting some really amazing paintings and working at the diner." He shook his head slowly, as if her work boggled his mind. "Added to that, you're beautiful and as sweet as you can be. You're pretty incredible, Liana Mann."

It took everything she had not to gape at him. Kent's short speech had been one of the nicest things anyone had ever told her. "Thank you."

He laughed.

Her cheeks heated. "I know. I'm completely awkward around you."

"Just around me?"

"Pretty much." And that was all she was going to admit to.

His smile slipped. "Do you still not trust me? Or is it something else? Did your husband mistreat you so badly that you're having a hard time believing anyone else?"

"I… I don't know." She half expected him to nod like he understood, but instead he stilled.

"I'd hate it if you didn't trust me, Liana. I'd never hurt you. I've never raised a hand to a woman in my life."

She almost smiled. "I can't imagine you ever hurting me." At least, not with his hands. But there was still a piece of her that wondered how genuine he was being. Did he really want to date her?

Or was it something else? Was he hoping to get closer to her so he could solve Billy's case?

"Have you discovered anything more?"

He blinked. "About your husband's murder?"

"Yes."

"Not really."

"But you did find out something?"

He leaned back. "I'd rather not talk about the case tonight."

She hadn't wanted to discuss it, either. But was that

really smart? She needed Billy's disappearance and murder solved as much as Kent did—but for far more personal reasons. She needed that part of her life to close so she could live again.

Taking a deep breath, she said, "When you reached out to me, there was no turning back. You know that, right?"

He stared at her, then smiled slowly. "I know that when we had coffee together there was something between us that had nothing to do with work. I want to explore it. But I'm not going to hide the fact that I'm working on your husband's cold case."

He'd spoken kindly, and his tone had been gentle. But he was also being completely honest and not hiding his determination to solve the case. "You're not going to let me stay in the dark anymore, are you?"

"No, I'm not." He swallowed, then said, "Don't take it personally, Liana. I realize that talking about your husband isn't easy. But we also can't ignore that I fully intend to charge someone for Billy's murder. I need your help and I need your perspective. I'm not going to let you hide things on purpose like you did with Officer Grune and Detective Evans. If you continue to hold back, it could jeopardize the outcome."

"I see." Even though his words made sense, she felt betrayed.

He still looked worried. Twin lines had appeared in between his brows. "Does that mean you understand?"

Deciding to be honest, as well, she said, "Not exactly. It means that I understand there's not a lot I can do right now. I wish there was."

He reached out for her hand. "You could hold my hand. You could try to trust me."

She linked her fingers through his. Smiled, too.

But all she could think was that he was going to have to trust her one day. She was going to have to try to trust him, too. However, Liana wondered if that was even possible. Would they ever be able to overcome all the odds against them to move forward?

She just wasn't sure.

Chapter Thirteen

"How's it going down in cold case world, Kent?" Jackson asked as they started their sixth lap jogging around the high school track.

He and Jackson used to be pretty good friends, though they'd had less and less in common over the past year. Jackson had been in the rookie class right behind him and had entered the force with the intention of making a name for himself—and it didn't seem like he had any regard for whose back or hard work he stepped on in order to make it happen.

As full of himself as Kent had once been, he'd never done that, and he didn't respect the men and women who did.

But even if he hadn't used people the way Jackson had, they'd drifted apart because Jackson reminded Kent a lot of the man he'd used to be. Back before his arrogance had cost a case and sent him down to the windowless cement confines of the basement.

However, they were fairly evenly matched runners, so every couple of weeks, Kent met him on the track to run. It was too bad that what used to be a form of

stress relief was now simply another source of aggravation in his life.

Like the way Jackson made no secret about the fact
that he was enjoying Kent's recent fall from grace.

"It's going," Kent finally said.

Jackson scoffed. "Come on. That's it? How's Crier?
I heard he's as ornery as an old rooster, always calling
you out and griping if you come in even a minute late."

"He's not that bad."

"Sure he's not."

Kent didn't appreciate his buddy's sarcasm, though
he was fairly sure Jackson's descriptor was dead-on.
Sergeant Crier really was ornery and ran the cold-case
division like the room of forgotten cases could get lost
if he didn't supervise each person from the moment
he or she dared to walk into his basement office. And,
since Kent was now there full-time, he got the brunt of
Sergeant Crier's constant guidance.

"Crier's all right. He's just set in his ways."

Jackson whistled under his breath. "You really are
taking the high road, aren't you?"

"I'm just trying to get through ten laps. That's all."
Actually, he was just trying to get through their current
conversation without slugging the guy.

Okay, he wasn't about to hit Jackson, but Kent was
tempted to give him an earful about how he felt about
all the nosy questions.

It wasn't that he minded talking about his new job,
per se, it was that he knew exactly why Jackson was
bringing it all up. Jackson was up for promotion to detective and was now practically buying suits that he
could wear as soon as he got out of his uniform every

day. When that happened, Jackson would get to laud that over Kent.

And there was no doubt in his mind that Jackson would do that.

Hoping to stop talking about work for a while, he said, "How's that gal you've been dating? What's her name... Avery?"

"She's fine." Sounding annoyed, Jackson added, "She dragged me into the jewelry store last weekend."

"Looking at rings, I guess?"

"Yep. Already."

That was kind of a surprise. "How long have you been dating?"

"Only seven months." His voice darkened. "I couldn't get out of that store fast enough."

"Guess she's anxious to get married. Or maybe she can't wait to lock you down so another woman won't snap you up."

Jackson chuckled. "Yeah...no. We get along fine and I really like her, but you know what happens when a gal hits twenty-eight."

"Nope."

"Once thirty is on the horizon, they start looking around and take stock of which friends are married, which ones have babies, which ones have good jobs... and which ones seem to be going nowhere. Avery's scared to death to be put in that last group."

He'd liked the woman when he met her. She smiled a lot and seemed to have no problem dealing with Jackson's ego. "I guess guys do the same thing...just a couple of years later."

He grinned. "Yeah, maybe. But if that's the case, then I guess I'm doing all right. I mean, I've got a good job, am about to have an even better one, and I've got a gal who can't wait to marry me."

Glad that they'd just completed the tenth lap, Kent slowed to a walk and veered off to the side so he could stretch. His hamstrings had been bothering him, and he'd pay big time if he didn't stretch.

"What about you?" Jackson asked. "Are you seeing anyone right now?"

He was reluctant to mention Liana. He not only liked to keep his private life private, but Kent also knew he was walking the line by spending time with Li while investigating her husband's death. All he needed was for Jackson to see it as a reason to report him.

"I'm not really seeing anyone," he finally said.

"Yeah, I guess it would be hard, given your demotion and all."

Kent felt like rolling his eyes. Of course Jackson had to get one more jab in before they said goodbye.

"Glad we fit this in tonight, Jackson. It was good to catch up."

"Hey, it's still early. Want to go grab a quick dinner maybe?"

"Sorry, I have other plans," Kent said. Looking at his phone, he frowned. "I've got to go. See you."

"Yeah, bye," Jackson said as he turned away.

Kent knew his coworker was annoyed with him, but he wasn't in the mood to try to soothe Jackson's vanity. He was too interested in what he was reading on his phone's screen.

Though he'd intended to use his phone as an excuse to get out of there fast, the text from his father made it a reality.

I found out something. Call me when you can.

* * *

As soon as he got to the car and turned on the air to cool things down, he called his dad. He answered immediately. "What's up?"

"I started thinking some more about Joe and some of the things he said, and then started digging through some of my old file boxes for my notes."

"What did you find?" There was no telling. His father was a product of his generation of detectives. They believed in paper, in saving it and didn't entirely trust files saved on flash drives.

"Brown and I had been working on a string of robberies and break-ins right around the time Billy Mann went missing. We'd taken Joe in for questioning the day before Billy vanished. We had enough circumstantial evidence to hold him overnight."

"So Joe couldn't be responsible."

"Right. In addition, the lieutenant assigned four officers to the area that whole week. They were everywhere, knocking on doors, patrolling all of Joe's buddies' usual hangouts. I'm not saying that I'm a hundred percent sure those guys didn't have anything to do with Billy's death…"

"But it doesn't seem likely," Kent finished.

"Exactly."

Sitting in his car, watching a couple of teenagers playing catch in a field nearby, Kent sighed. He'd been holding out a vague hope that Billy's death had been a drug-related crime. But from the first, it hadn't felt that way. Now it looked like there was another reason to believe that line was a dead end. "Thanks for all your help, Dad."

"Hey, you sound discouraged."

"I'm not. Sergeant Crier has told me often that there's a reason cold cases were never solved. They're tricky, right?" He smiled, hoping his father realized he was speaking a little tongue-in-cheek.

"They are, but I have faith in you, Kent."

"Thanks a lot."

Obviously, his father could hear the slight sarcasm in his tone. "No, listen. I'm serious. You might have made some mistakes in the past, but you've also done a lot of good. You're a good cop and you've got a lot of heart. That's going to see you through this. I promise."

"Thanks, Dad," he said again, but this time meaning it completely. "I think I needed to hear that today."

"Oh, Kent. *All* of us need to hear it from time to time. If you ever can't believe in yourself, you've got to remember that other people do. Just like the Lord does."

Kent thought about those words the whole way home.

Chapter Fourteen

Liana wasn't sure why she'd agreed to come to her brother, Mason, and Jeanie's backyard barbecue. She supposed it had to do with all the tales Kent had shared about his family.

However, just ten minutes in, Liana knew accepting the invitation had been a mistake. Mason was acting kind of odd and Jeanie was pretending he wasn't. Then, to make matters worse, they'd invited another couple over. Brenda had been in the same graduating class at Western Hills High School as Liana but they'd never been close. Things had even gotten more strained between them when Brenda had married well and moved into a big house in the Cincinnati suburbs. Liana didn't care what Brenda did, but whenever they'd run into each other, Brenda had made sure that Liana knew they were now in different social circles.

Though maybe not, since Brenda and her husband, Doug had obviously known that Mason had invited Liana to the shindig.

Now, while the guys were grilling brats and chicken, Liana was stuck sitting with Brenda and Jeanie. Brenda and Jay's two preschool-age kids were running around the yard with Mason's dog, Spot.

"Are you sure you don't want any more root beer, Li?" Jeanie asked.

"I'm positive. Water's fine with me."

"Or another appetizer?"

The appetizers were little smokies rolled up in crescent rolls. They were tasty but she'd already had three of them. "Jeanie, I promise, I'm good. Plus, you don't have to wait on me. You know that."

"I know…"

Brenda chuckled. "You should let her fuss, Liana. I mean, this is probably the first time in ages that you haven't been the one waiting on other people."

Liana knew Brenda had probably meant to sound disparaging, but she didn't see it that way. She honestly really did like waiting tables at the diner and wasn't about to be embarrassed about it. Summoning a smile, she looked at Brenda. "You're probably right."

Looking slightly surprised that Liana had taken her comment so well, Brenda cleared her throat. "So how are things at the diner?"

"They're good. I bet you're keeping busy with the kids."

"Oh, yes. Both Crane and Lincoln are in preschool now. Next year Crane will be in kindergarten. I don't know where the years ago."

She'd often felt the same way, though when she reflected on the time, it was about how much she'd wasted. She'd spent too many years trying to make Billy into something he wasn't, and even longer than that living in limbo while he'd been missing.

"You are blessed to have such a nice family, Brenda. I'm happy for you."

"I am blessed. Thank you."

As the stilted conversation drew to a stop, Jeanie crossed her legs. "Hey, Li, have you ever told Brenda about your painting?"

"I'm not sure," she replied, though Liana knew for a fact that she would've never talked about her paintings with Brenda.

Brenda's eyebrows rose over the rims of her sunglasses. "What kind of painting are you doing? Interiors?"

Before Liana could answer, Jeanie said, "You should see these monster paintings she makes, Brenda. They're big, like three feet by four feet."

"Really? What are they of?"

"Nothing," Jeanie said. "Right, Li?"

She couldn't really say that they were of nothing. In her mind the abstracts were representations of all kinds of things. Emotions, recollections, dreams. "They're abstract pieces."

Brenda's brows pulled together. "You mean they're just a bunch of colorful blobs?"

"I guess some might see them that way. I don't, however."

"I don't, either," Jeanie interjected quickly. "I love your paintings, Li."

"Thanks." Smiling at her sister-in-law, Liana almost felt like chuckling. She could sense the embarrassment and regret pouring off Jeanie's shoulders as she watched her conversational effort go down in flames.

Brenda's voice turned sweet as sugarcane. "Liana, no offense, but when are you ever going to get your life together?"

"I beg your pardon?"

"Come on. You married *Billy Mann*." Brenda's voice rose. "He was a total jerk, then he went missing. For years!"

"Why are you acting like that was either his or my fault?"

Brenda waved a manicured hand. "All I'm saying is that you wasted years just sitting around and waiting for Billy to show up again. It's sad, really."

While Liana fumed, Jeanie placed a hand on Brenda's arm. "Brenda, I think you've crossed the line."

"Do you really think so? If so, then I'm sorry. Truly, I'm just curious. I know I'm not the only one from our group of friends who feels this way, either."

"He was murdered, Brenda," Liana said.

Jeanie frowned. "Are you sure about that, hon? I thought maybe the cops believed that he'd been out hiking and fell or something."

Liana couldn't believe that she was having to share all of this in the middle of a barbecue. "First of all, Billy didn't hike. Secondly, they found marks on his spine. His neck had been broken. Someone killed him."

"Where did you hear that?" Mason asked.

Surprised, Liana turned to her brother. Mason was standing with Brenda's husband, Jay. But while Jay was merely listening with a curious expression on his face, her brother looked almost angry.

"I heard it from the cop who's in charge of his case, Mason."

"What case?" He scoffed. "Billy's been dead a long time. What happened to him doesn't matter. Not really, right?"

The callous way her brother was speaking caught Liana off guard. While it was true that Billy had been horrible to her in countless ways, she hadn't ever wished he'd been murdered. No one should be killed the way he'd been and then forgotten about for a decade.

"I think you're wrong, Mason." Not caring anymore that she was airing her dirty laundry in front of Brenda and Jay, she added, "Even though Billy abused me and I've wished I never married him, I can't be all right with the way he died. No one's life should be seen as disposable."

"You don't know what you're talking about. I don't even understand why you're talking to the cops." He scowled. "Honestly, Li, I don't understand why you would ever even think about Billy again. It would be a lot better for you if you just forgot he ever existed."

She knew then that she'd probably never share with Mason the things Martha had taught her about forgiveness. Forgiving was an essential part of the Amish life. Though Liana would never be Amish, of course, she had accepted that forgiving others' transgressions brought peace. It didn't matter if they deserved to be forgiven or not—that was up to God.

So she would keep that to herself. But there were still other questions that Mason's words and attitude brought to mind. For example, it was hard not to ask him why he was so eager to keep Billy's case closed.

Hoping to ease the tension between them, she said, "I think we should talk about this another day, Mason."

"Honey, is lunch ready?" Jeanie asked brightly.

Mason's angry expression slowly faded. "Yeah. That's what we came in here to tell you. Let's eat."

"I'm starving," Brenda said as she walked to her husband's side. "I'll go help the kids wash up."

When only the two of them were standing together, Mason stopped Liana. Concern etched his features. "Li, I'm sorry. I shouldn't have acted so fired up." He rubbed a hand over his face. "It's just that sometimes, I can hardly bear to think about how badly he hurt you. I practically see red every time I hear his name. I wish you'd just put him in the past."

"I didn't bring him up, Mason. Brenda did. Then Jeanie acted like he'd just gotten hurt in some hiking accident. Since I know that isn't true, I corrected her."

When he continued to frown at her, she said, "What's going on? You look upset with me."

"I'm not upset… I think you should just let sleeping dogs lie."

"I want the truth, Mason. Besides, the cop in charge of the investigation wants to solve it. He's not going to give up."

"Sounds like you know a lot about what he wants. How come?"

"Why do you think? I've talked to him a lot. I'm trying to help."

"No cop did much when Billy went missing, except question you. That Detective Evans was a jerk and barely ever returned your calls when you called to see if he'd made any progress. You don't need to help them now."

"This police officer is different. K—I mean, Officer Olson is a good man. He really cares about solving this case."

"Going back over things that happened a decade ago

isn't going to help you, Liana." His voice turned husky with emotion. "All it's going to do is dredge up a lot of bad memories."

"Mason, I love you, and I've appreciated how you've looked after me for years. I don't know what I would've done without your help…especially when I was still with Billy. But you don't need to worry about me anymore. I'm stronger now."

"You know where you'd be if I hadn't helped you, Li? You'd be in the ground somewhere. That's what would've happened to you. Billy wasn't going to stop beating you and he wasn't ever going to let you go."

"I guess it's good that God stepped in and took care of him, then."

"God and whoever had the good sense to give Billy what he had coming. Only the good Lord and Billy's murderer helped you live, Liana. Remember that next time you're trying to be oh so helpful to a bunch of cops," he threw over his shoulder as he walked into the kitchen.

He let the door slam behind him. It gave Liana a good minute to catch her breath. She'd just felt as if her brother was giving her a warning—but about what?

Was he really concerned about her turning back into the beaten woman that she'd been? Was he really that upset about her trying to help solve Billy's murder? Or was it something more?

Remembering the day Billy went missing, the expression on Mason's face when he'd seen just how banged up she'd been when he stopped by her house unexpectedly, Liana finally allowed herself to face her worst fear. That Mason knew a whole lot more about the night Billy had been killed than he'd ever let on.

If that was the truth, she had to figure out what to do about it. Did she keep it to herself, confront her brother about her suspicions or tell everything to Kent?

She honestly didn't know.

Chapter Fifteen

Liana had been stewing and praying about what to do for a while now. If she kept to herself, she felt safer. She could paint, read her books, lie to herself and pretend nothing was wrong. She sure had lots of practice doing that.

On the other hand, she could reach out to Kent and talk to him about what was on her mind. If she did that, she would risk opening her past up to more questions. And perhaps even risk their new friendship. After all, Kent might think he really liked her—but what if he learned things that he didn't like? He would eventually finish his investigation and she would never hear from him again.

Frustrated with herself, she walked to her front flower beds and started weeding. Pulling weeds wasn't going to change her life, but at least she'd get something done while she fretted.

"Look at ya, working hard in the sun today!" Martha called as she trotted up the walkway.

Tossing the weed she'd just removed on the ground, Liana stood up to face her sweet Amish neighbor. "Hi,

Martha! This is a nice surprise. I haven't seen you in days."

Martha set down the basket she was holding. "Sol and me have been on vacation. It was our twenty-fifth anniversary."

"Twenty-five years? Congratulations. That's wonderful."

"*Danke. Got* has been *gut* to us. We are blessed."

Liana smiled. "You two deserve many blessings. You are wonderful people." When Martha just chuckled, Liana added, "So where did you two go?"

"We went on a bus trip to Shipshy."

"You went out to Indiana? Good for you. Did you go to the flea market?"

"We did, but we mainly saw our friends." Still looking pleased, Martha said, "It was a *gut* trip."

Since she couldn't stop thinking about Kent, Liana asked, "Do you have any relationship advice?"

"Do you need some?"

"Kind of." Feeling Martha's steady gaze on her, she sighed. "I mean, yes."

"If you are walking into a relationship, then I'm happy for ya."

"So any advice?"

She folded her arms and looked out into the distance. "Well, I suppose I could tell ya to be honest and patient with each other. Hmm. And that humor is always a good thing, too…" She clucked her tongue. "But I reckon the best advice is to believe in love."

"Believe in love?" Liana didn't even try to hide her incredulity. "That doesn't sound very Amishy, Martha."

Martha chuckled. "Maybe it is, maybe it ain't. All I

do know is if one doesn't believe in love, it makes for a real hard marriage."

"I guess you have a point."

Martha grinned. "Of course I do." Picking up the basket, she said, "I brought you some of my first berries and a loaf of sourdough."

Taking the basket from her, Liana smiled. "Thank you. I will enjoy both of them."

"*Gut*. Now, I'd best get on home and you'd better go do whatever it is you were putting off."

"Weeding?"

Martha chuckled again as she started walking down the path. "Weeds will wait, Liana. Go do what's really on your mind, *ja*?"

"*Ja*," she whispered back. When Martha was out of sight, Liana carried the basket back inside, popped a sun-warmed blackberry into her mouth and picked up her cell phone at last.

Her wise neighbor was right. It was time to stop fussing around. Afraid to waste another moment, she dialed the number she now had memorized.

"Liana, is this really you?" Kent teased the moment he answered.

Surprised, Liana frowned at her cell phone's screen. "Yes. Why?"

"Because this is the first time you've called me. I just wanted to make sure no one had picked it up and started dialing."

Finally catching on to his playfulness, she rolled her eyes. "If I would have known you would be so entertaining when you picked up, I would've called you weeks ago."

"Sorry. I'm just pleased. So what's up?"

Looking at Martha's basket, she took a fortifying breath. "Well, um, I thought maybe we should talk about something."

"This sounds serious." All traces of humor faded from his voice. "I'm sorry for joking around. Did you call about the case? Have you remembered something new?"

"No. This isn't about the case," she said in a rush. "I mean, it kind of is, but not really."

"What is it about?"

"You and me."

"Come again?"

Kent sounded completely baffled and Liana didn't blame him. Boy, she was making a mess of things. "Sorry. I'm not making any sense. Let me backtrack. See, I went to my brother's house for a barbecue yesterday." She paused again, trying to find the right way to convey a bunch of things she wasn't even sure she wanted to say out loud.

"You went to Mason's," he prodded after a couple of seconds went by.

"Yes." A knot formed in her stomach. She knew they'd talked about Mason but it kind of took her off guard how easily Kent had recalled her brother's name. Feeling even more awkward, she continued. "Well, you see, my sister-in-law, Jeanie, had first been hoping to set me up with a friend of theirs when I was there, but it ended up just being a get-together with some friends."

"Okay." That one word sounded as strained as she felt.

She closed her eyes. Why had she decided to call him without practicing first?

Because it was the right thing to do, she reminded

herself. "Well, um, to be honest, the barbecue was kind of a bust. An old friend was there who isn't really very nice. She brought up Billy, which of course led to her talking about how bad he'd treated me. And then…well, then I told everyone that he'd been murdered."

"I see."

Kent didn't sound too happy. "I didn't think Billy's murder was a secret," she murmured. "Was it?"

"No. I mean, I wouldn't have told you if it couldn't be shared." His voice sounded carefully controlled.

"Good. Okay, then," she murmured, but she felt like she was talking in circles.

"Anyway, everyone was pretty shocked by that news, and then my brother got kind of upset with me about you."

"What did you say about me?"

"Not much. Only that you're different from the other cops." When Kent didn't respond right away, she attempted again to be more articulate. "I meant that you've been helpful and that I've been helping you." She closed her eyes, wishing she didn't sound so nervous and awkward. "I mean, that we're working together."

"That's true. We are working together," Kent replied, sounding as if he was weighing every word. "But Mason didn't like hearing that?"

"No." Liana took a deep breath, ready to share her suspicions about Mason knowing more than he was letting on, but she chickened out. "He thinks Detective Evans and Officer Grune should have worked harder on the case. He believes they should have called to give me more updates."

"I don't think there's anything wrong with your brother feeling that way," Kent said. "He cares about you. I'd feel the same way about my sister." Sounding slightly amused, he added, "Li, don't worry about him hurting my feelings, either. I can take it."

She sighed. "Kent, that isn't the whole reason I called."

"What else is on your mind?"

"When I told them that we were working together, I didn't mention our date."

"Because you thought they'd be upset?"

"Yes." Because he was a cop. "I enjoyed our date. I liked it a lot." She felt happy just thinking about the loving glances, the way he'd taken her hand, his lips on her cheek… "I thought it went well. Did you feel the same?"

"I did. I absolutely did." He sighed. "But to be honest, everything that you mentioned has crossed my mind, too. It might be a good idea if we slowed things down a bit. After all, I'm investigating a case which you have ties to."

A new worry crossed her mind. "You don't think I'm a suspect, do you?"

He chuckled. "As bad as you think Officer Grune and Detective Evans were, they ruled you out as a suspect. There's no worries there."

"Good."

"But even though I believe you're perfectly innocent, some might see our relationship as a conflict of interest for me."

He still sounded so controlled, Liana couldn't get a read on his mood. Boy, she wished she would've waited to talk to him in person. "What do you think we should do, Kent?"

"I want to keep you as a friend. And when all of this

is over, I'd like for us to take things to a more romantic place. That is, if you still feel the same way."

"All right. I think that sounds smart."

"Don't worry. I have a feeling all this will be over with soon."

"Really? Did you find out something new?"

"Nothing that I can share. But I have been talking to some of your husband's old friends. We're getting some good information."

"I guess that's the most I'm going to get to hear about right now, huh?"

He chuckled. "You sound irritated. Please, don't be. I promise I'm on your side."

"I'll have to trust you, I guess…"

"Does that mean if I ask you out for pizza tonight you'll say yes?"

She felt like he was being hot and cold and she couldn't keep up. "What about our decision to step back and avoid conflicts of interest?"

"Even friends go out for pizza, Liana. What do you say?"

After weighing the pros and cons and remembering Martha's words of advice, she said, "Could we meet in Anderson instead of out here by my house? I… I'd rather not take a chance on Mason seeing us together."

"That's fine with me. Panjo's Pizza is just a couple of blocks from my work. How about we meet there?"

"I can do that."

"Great. Say, six o'clock?"

"Six sounds good. Thank you, Kent."

"No, thank you. I'm really glad you called," he said in a warmer tone of voice. "You were right to bring all this up, Liana. I should've brought it up when we went to dinner but I was having such a good time I didn't want anything to spoil it. We need to keep everything out in the open and talk about anything that's bothering us. It's better that way." She heard a beep. "Oh, sorry. I've got to take this. See you at six. Bye."

He hung up before she could say another word, which was probably a good thing. At this moment she wasn't sure how she felt about anything.

Popping another blackberry into her mouth, she amended that thought. She might not be sure how she felt about a lot of things, but she was sure of one thing—Martha had been right. It was better to believe in love—or at least in the possibility of it happening one day.

Chapter Sixteen

"I can't believe you talked me into this," Liana said a week after their dinner at Panjo's. After several days of exchanging texts, phone calls and even one quick breakfast at the diner, he'd convinced her to do something she never thought she would—attend one of her gallery showings at Gallery One.

"I didn't talk you into anything," Kent said. "You made up your mind on your own."

"Not exactly." Folding her hands together in her lap, she added, "I seem to remember you making me feel pretty guilty about always refusing Serena."

After changing lanes a couple of times on the highway, he darted a smile her way. "All I did was point out that this evening could be fun." When she coughed, he added, "And that Serena would probably be extremely grateful for your presence."

Though she knew that Serena was grateful, Liana doubted she was going to find any part of the evening fun. That said, she thought she might feel pretty proud of herself. She needed to take more chances and have more confidence in herself. Going to this party would be another step in the right direction.

When Liana didn't say anything for several seconds, Kent's teasing grin faded. "Wait, you really don't want to go, do you?"

"I really don't, Kent. But you knew that."

He flicked on his turn signal and started moving toward the exit. She held on for her life. "What are you doing? And by the way, do all cops drive like you?"

"I'm taking the next exit. We'll go do something else." Glancing at her again, he chuckled. "And yes. Most of the cops I know drive like this. It's part of the job."

Realizing that he was being completely serious, she glared at him. "Wait! We can't back out. Serena would kill me. And I didn't realize putting your life on the line on the highway was a requirement for employment."

"Most cops have put hours and hours on duty on the highways. We're pretty comfortable there." He switched lanes again. "You can blame your absence on me, Liana. Tell Serena I changed my mind or that something came up and I couldn't attend."

"I'm not going to blame anything on you."

"You can if you'd like. After all, I'm the one who pushed you to do this in the first place. It wasn't right and I should've respected your wishes more."

"No, I'm going to do this." If she backed out now she'd never forgive herself.

Kent glanced at her again. "Are you sure?"

"I'm sure." She meant it, too. "I just don't like crowds. Or strangers."

"No kidding?"

Liana attempted to look affronted, but really all she

could think was that she was comfortable with him. Here they were, having two conversations at the same time and joking while they were doing it. That wasn't anything she was used to—but she couldn't deny that she was enjoying every minute of it.

Fifteen minutes later Kent pulled into one of the last spots in the parking lot. It was off to the side, but it did afford her a view through one of the large plate-glass windows. The gallery was brightly lit. The white walls were in stark contrast to the black metal crown molding and the chrome fixtures attached to the ceiling. It all looked modern and slightly cold. Actually, Liana had often thought it looked much like a prison for paintings.

But she'd never seen her paintings displayed on the walls at night. Or when there were customers in the space.

"Whoa," Kent said. "Your paintings look amazing, Li."

"They really do." She couldn't deny it—her paintings looked gorgeous. Their bold, vivid colors looked cheerful and welcoming compared to the dark storefronts surrounding the gallery.

"There's a ton of people in there, too. And every one of them is dressed to the nines just to see your work." He winked.

She knew he was impressed with the fancy crowd and likely was trying to make her feel excited about it, too. But all she could do at the moment was stare at her outfit in dismay. "Do you see those ladies' cocktail dresses? I'm in black slacks and a white polyester blouse." She moaned. "They're going to think I'm their waiter."

He opened the driver's-side door and stepped out. "If they do, then they won't say a word to you—other than they'd like a glass of champagne or something. You won't have a thing to be worried about."

He had her there. Just as Liana reached for her door handle, he was already there. He had a hand out to help her to her feet.

She took it, once again realizing that no one had ever treated her like he did. It wasn't so much the compliments and flowers as much as knowing that she mattered.

And Liana couldn't deny it—she loved that she mattered to him.

He kept her hand encased in his, using his other to close her door and click the lock with his key fob. "So what's the plan?"

"First, find Serena. Second, talk her out of making me give a speech."

"Sounds good."

"That's it?"

Kent looked at her in confusion. "What do you mean?"

"Come on. You usually have so much to say about everything. I thought you were going to give me tons of tips all night."

"Nope. I have lots to say about police work. Precious little about gallery openings—especially not to the talented artist herself."

"Thanks."

"No problem." He leaned closer. "Besides, I'll have you know that I'm already feeling pretty great about tonight."

"Why is that?"

He lifted her hand to his mouth and kissed her knuckles. "Because I'm with the prettiest girl in the room. You look beautiful, Liana. I promise."

She was so touched, she didn't even bother to remind him that they were just friends. "Not waiter-like?"

"Oh, absolutely like a waiter. No doubt about that. But you're the prettiest one around."

Her bark of laughter floated to the door he opened, causing several people to look their way. The ladies smiled at her.

Liana smiled back.

Then couldn't help but giggle as she caught sight of Serena, who was gaping at her like she'd seen a ghost. After whispering something to the man she was talking to, she rushed forward, her dark black hair swishing along the middle of her back and contrasting with the red satin fabric of her dress.

"Liana Mann! You're here!"

And just like that, the room went silent. She could practically feel every pair of eyes focus on her. She felt her hand shake and hated herself right then for showing up.

Then, just as she was about to whisper to Kent to get her out of there, the whole room erupted into applause.

Every person was clapping.

"Look at that," Kent whispered. "That's for you."

She was stunned. "I don't know what to do."

"Stand and smile and take it in. You've earned it."

She couldn't think of anything to say to that, but she supposed it didn't matter because Serena was enfolding her in her arms. "Thank you, Liana. Thank you so much. You being here is amazing. No, it's better than that. It's…it's everything!"

When she pulled back, Liana was caught off guard by the emotion in her friend's eyes. Serena really wasn't exaggerating. She was ecstatic about Li being there. "I almost asked Kent to turn around but he convinced me to be brave," she confided.

"No, Liana decided that on her own." He held his hand out. "Kent Olson. Pleasure to meet you."

"I'm Serena Ketels, and it's very nice to meet you, too."

"Are you ever going to let this lady loose so we can talk to her, Serena?" an elderly man asked.

"One second, Frank." Turning to Liana again, Serena lowered her voice. "I'm thrilled you're here, but I don't want you to be miserable. How do you want to handle this? You can visit with people or talk for ten or fifteen minutes about your work to everyone."

"Which is easier?"

"The talk will get almost everything out of the way, while the chatting would take longer but is kind of fun. It's up to you."

Looking at the couple waiting so expectantly, she realized that she wouldn't be able to simply walk away. "I guess I'll chat."

"Okay, I'll announce that."

Suddenly everything—her art on the walls, the fact that there were a ton of people all staring at her, even this elderly man named Frank who seemed ready to ask her a ton of questions—all seemed so real. "Will you stay nearby?"

"I will…but I'm also going to be selling paintings."

"I won't leave your side, Liana," Kent whispered.

When she smiled up at him and spied the assurance in his blue eyes, she felt her whole body relax. That was when she knew that while she might be Kent's key to a cold case he was desperate to solve, and they might be friends, there was something far more between them than those two things.

For better or worse, Kent had become very important to her. So important that she wasn't going to ever want to let him go.

Chapter Seventeen

Kent was so proud of her. During the past two hours, Liana had talked to dozens of strangers about her paintings. She posed for pictures with them. She talked about her inspiration for different works and didn't so much as hesitate when asked to write a personal message on the back of a canvas to several buyers.

Little by little, she'd come into her own—at least Kent thought so. At first, she'd looked petrified and constantly seemed to glance his way, to make sure that he hadn't left her side. But he'd meant what he'd promised. He'd hovered and been ready to help her out if someone asked anything too intrusive.

But Liana hadn't needed him.

Serena had stayed close, too, though she'd been actively selling paintings like the pro that she was. Not that it seemed to be too hard to make sales. Everyone in attendance was enthralled by Liana's work and acted as if the opportunity to actually speak to her about her paintings was an amazing gift.

By the second hour, Liana had relaxed enough to sip on some peppermint tea he'd found for her. Her smile appeared more easily, and her replies to customers' questions sounded less forced.

Then, true to her word, Serena closed the show promptly at nine o'clock. When the last couple was leaving—after buying two of her largest canvases—Liana whispered that she had to run to the bathroom.

Glad to take a breather, he walked around the room, taking notice of the bright gold SOLD signs that were now attached to over half of the canvases. Given the prices they were marked at, Kent figured Liana had just made an amazing amount of money.

It was incredible.

"Kent, I'd marry you if I could," Serena declared after locking the front door.

"I'm flattered, but I don't think your offer has much to do with my good looks and charm as much as the company I keep."

She grinned at him appreciatively. "Though you aren't anything to sneeze at, you would be right. I'm forever in your debt because you were able to get Liana here. You have no idea how surprised I was to see her."

No way was he going to take so much credit. "Liana wanted to come."

"Ah, we both know that she did not."

"Okay, how about this… I think she was finally curious enough about the show to not fight too hard about coming. She did great, too."

Serena broke into a wide smile. "Liana did better than great. She was so down-to-earth and humble, everyone was completely charmed. They fell in love with her at first sight." Looking at the many paintings with sold signs, she added, "And they showed their appreciation with their pocketbooks."

Kent couldn't deny that he was slightly shocked by Liana's success. "I had no idea she was so well-known."

"That's the thing. She isn't well-known, but her work is well loved. There's a difference, you know. Plus, she's fabulous."

"She is that."

"Are you two talking about me?" Liana asked as she joined them.

"We absolutely are," Serena said. "How could we not? You were the star of the show tonight."

Liana's cheeks pinkened as she shook her head like she was a little dazed. "I still don't know what to think about it all. You were incredible, Serena. I'm glad I got to see you in action. And I feel pretty bad that I wasn't here before."

Smiling at Kent, Serena said, "Actually, I think it was better that you weren't. Everyone felt like they were attending a really special event. There's a time and a place for everything, Liana. I think this just happened to be your night."

"Maybe so."

Serena darted a look from Kent to Liana and back again. "Any chance one of you wants to tell me what is going on with you two?"

"Nope," Kent said.

"We're just friends," Liana murmured.

"Oh, obviously."

As Liana picked up a pair of clear plastic cups, Serena practically batted her hand away. "No, you don't. I'm going to do the cleanup. You two um, good friends can get on your way."

"We can't leave you with this mess," Liana protested.

"I agree," Kent said. "You've got to be as tired as Liana."

Serena tossed a chunk of her dark hair over one shoulder. "If you think tonight has worn me out, you've got a big surprise coming your way. I haven't felt so jazzed in weeks. I'll be fine. I won't be able to sleep for another couple of hours even if I tried."

"Are you sure?"

"I've got some help coming in early tomorrow. They're going to help me crate and ship paintings to some and hand deliver the others. Along the way we're going to be cleaning. I promise I've got it covered." She made a shooing motion with her hands. "That means the two of you need to get on out of here and go celebrate."

Kent thought that was a great idea. "What do you think, Liana? Are you ready to sit down and relax for a bit?"

"I guess so. You might not be tired, but I feel like I just ran a marathon."

"Be careful going out. It's usually pretty safe around here, but every once in a while someone is lurking."

"Kent's a cop. We'll be fine."

Serena raised her eyebrows. "Is that right? Now, isn't this a night for surprises?"

Kent didn't even want to try to decipher that comment. "I'd feel better if we stayed and I walked you out, too."

"Thanks, but I've got a guy who's a *friend*, too. He's coming to pick me up in an hour." She held up a hand. "I promise."

Feeling like he'd done as much as he could for Serena, he turned to Liana. "Ready to take off?"

"Almost." She hugged Serena tight. "Thank you so

much for everything. I know there's more to say but I have no words."

"Given it's you, sweetheart, I'd say that's no surprise. Take care of our girl," she said to Kent after she shook his hand. "She's pretty special."

"Always," he murmured as he took Liana's hand and led her outside. He smiled to himself, enjoying the way she still seemed to be in a little dream world.

After helping her buckle up and then getting in on his side, he leaned over and kissed her lightly.

Her eyes widened. "What was that for?"

"No reason. It was just um…a friendship kiss."

She giggled. "Yes, I'm sure there are some friends who kiss all the time." Yawning, she leaned back in her seat as he pulled out of the parking lot. "I'm too tired to argue about that…especially since I'm so glad you made me do this and that you stayed by my side."

"I didn't want to be anywhere else. Promise. Now, since it's half past nine, our choices for dinner are pretty limited. What are you hungry for?"

"Any kind of fast food is fine."

"Are you sure?" He was pretty certain that the last time he'd bought a date fast food he'd been in high school.

"Of course." She smiled at him. "I'm not picky."

Deciding that she might not be picky but she was probably starving, he pulled over to the first place he saw—the inevitable golden arches. It was late enough that only the drive through was available. Instead of apologizing again, he went with it and asked what she wanted, then ordered two of everything.

Then he pulled into one of the many empty parking spaces, handed her a soda and started pulling out burgers and fries.

"Oh, yum," she said just before taking a big bite.

He laughed, thinking that her appreciation echoed his own to a T. "This does taste pretty good."

"I think all that nervous energy got the best of me. This tastes *so* good."

She wasn't wrong. Ten minutes later he tossed their trash in a receptacle and headed back on the highway.

Next to him Liana looked completely relaxed and sated. So much so that he decided to finally ask her something that had been bugging him ever since he'd realized just how successful she'd been that evening.

"Hey, Li?"

"Hmm?"

"Why aren't you doing this full-time?"

"Doing what? Sitting in the passenger seat while you drive me around places?"

"You know what I mean. Painting. You obviously love it, and you've got a lot of people who love your work. And you make good money."

Her lazy countenance evaporated into wariness. "I don't—"

"Come on. I know you know how much those paintings are going for."

"Tonight was a fluke."

Was she in denial or just extremely modest? Or maybe the reality was that she didn't want to discuss it with him. Thinking that was most likely the case, he nodded. "Oh, okay. Your exit is up ahead."

Taking the exit, he veered right and headed down the state highway toward her home. Even though it was just a little after ten o'clock, the road was essentially deserted.

The car was dark. Only passing headlights and an occasional streetlamp illuminated her face. He would have loved to get a feel for what she was thinking. But maybe he should be grateful for her secrets. He was in no position to give her advice, especially since she wasn't asking for it in the first place.

No, what he should have done was keep his mouth shut. Thinking of his arrogance, of the way he'd almost ruined his career, Kent felt his cheeks burn. When was he going to learn to listen? The Lord was probably wondering that exact same thing, as well.

"I'm afraid."

The words seemed so bare, vulnerable, maybe even more forceful in the dark.

His mouth went dry as he weighed different responses. But since none of them would do, he elected to simply speak from his heart.

"I understand."

"You do?"

"Well, I know what it's like to be afraid. Fear is pretty hard to overcome, hard to ignore. I'd say it's pretty powerful."

"It is." When he kept silent, she added, "Sometimes, when I'm really being honest with myself, I know what the root of it is."

"What?"

He could almost see her lick her bottom lip. Glance at him warily...analyze the pros and cons of trusting him.

"I'm afraid to believe in myself," she said at last.

"I've had that same fear," he admitted.

"Really? How did you make peace with it?"

How? He was currently working in the basement of the police department, unsure if he was ever going to have what it took to claw his way out. He was constantly comparing himself to his father and knowing that he would never be as good, respected or smart.

Now, as he tried so hard to improve his reputation, what did he do? He was starting to fall for the one woman he shouldn't. Worse, he was afraid to tell her all that on the chance that she would decide she didn't want another thing to do with him.

"I haven't," he said at last. "I haven't made peace with a thing. But I believe hope is powerful."

"Hope is everything, Kent."

They rode in silence the rest of the way to her house.

He was breaking up with her. "I see. So you want to not see each other anymore?"

"What? No. No!" He groaned. "See, this is why I have as many hang-ups as you do. I overthink things. Then, when I finally do get the nerve to do what's on my mind, it comes out in a heap of complicated gibberish."

She chuckled. "Maybe not that bad."

"It feels like it." He sighed. "Anyway, what I'm trying to say is that while there are a lot of good reasons to wait and be cautious, I'm tired of letting all of my fears rule my actions."

"Okay…" she said, hoping that he would give her some more information and not leave her hanging there.

When he exhaled, she could practically feel his frustration with himself. "Liana, what I'm trying to say is that I want you to come over to my parents' house with me for Sunday dinner."

"Sunday dinner?"

"I always go over there on Sunday nights. Don't say no. It's casual. Well, pretty casual, I mean for them. What do you say?"

"I say…what?"

"Uh-oh. What did I do now?"

"You're talking in circles, Kent." She felt like he'd gone from point A to B to the letter M in one fell swoop. "We agreed a few days ago that our seeing each other was a conflict of interest. Then we were going to be just friends but then you kissed me. And now you've decided to stop living in fear and your solution is to eat dinner with your parents?"

"Okay, I know I might sound like I don't know what I want. But I do."

would mean that she'd have to stop hiding behind the bright artwork and come into her own. But…was she really brave enough to hold her head up high and look people like Brenda in the eye and say that she was an artist? Would she really be able to admit to her brother that she was no longer living on the outskirts of poverty but dancing in the shadows of all their dreams? She didn't know. Billy had left her a massive amount of scars, both physical and emotional. But while faint white lines from his various injuries marred her body, they weren't the ones that still hurt. No, the injuries that still seared her soul had come from his emotional abuse. The lies. The way he'd always made her feel less than she was.

Tonight's visit to the gallery was evidence of that.

Then there was Kent. What was going on with them? Yes, they were just friends now, but she knew as much as he did that they weren't fooling anyone with that label. Least of all themselves.

When her phone rang, she stared at it in confusion before picking it up. "Kent?"

"Yeah, it's me." He sounded disgruntled. "Sorry it's so late. Did I wake you up?"

"No. I was um, just sitting here on the couch." No reason to tell him about the half-demolished cake still perched on her lap. "Is everything okay? Did you make it home okay?"

"Hmm? Oh, yeah. I've been home for a while."

"That's good."

"Listen, the whole way home, I was thinking about us, and about fear and all the reasons that we should probably wait to take things further."

Chapter Nineteen

Kent had prepped his parents before their arrival, but he didn't know if it had done a lot of good. Dad had sounded amused on the phone and barely stayed on five minutes before passing it on to his mother. Kent had watched his father practice that move all his life. There was a reason his father had risen so high in the ranks of the police department, and it was his ability to step away before he said or did something inappropriate.

Dad had put that habit into play with his parents and in-laws plenty of times. Even the Bennetts, the annoying neighbors who'd moved in from Maryland and then moved out again ten months later, citing that Cincinnati, Ohio, was just far too quaint for someone with their East Coast roots.

And now his father had played that same game with him.

Not Mom, though. Mom had been determined to speak her mind, all of which was focused on her son's mistaken impression that she wouldn't be welcoming to his new girlfriend.

Kent had hung up with the feeling that he'd made

an error, but he couldn't quite put his finger on what, exactly, he'd done wrong.

Now, as he was pulling into his parents' driveway with Liana by his side, he was hoping he was a better actor than parent-prepper. Liana looked so nervous she was practically shaking, and simply holding her hand wasn't making things any better.

"Liana, I promise, they're nice people and they're excited to meet you."

But she kept staring at the front of the house. "You said your father was a cop, just like you."

"That's true."

"Then how come y'all have this?" She waved a hand toward the black front door.

"It's just a house, Li."

"No, it's a really *big* house."

He felt like pointing out that she could probably get herself a pretty fine-looking house with the money she'd been stashing in her bank account, but knew that wouldn't go over too well. "Both of my parents have worked hard all their lives. Plus, Dad inherited some money when his father died. That's how they have this."

"So it's family money."

She made it sound like he was a trust-fund kid, and he wasn't that. Not at all. However, he was beginning to realize that anything he said wouldn't come across right. Taking her other hand in his, he added, "Liana, I promise none of this matters all that much. It's just a house. What matters is the people inside, and I can tell you with a hundred percent certainty that both of my parents are currently peeking out the window and wondering why we aren't coming in."

"You think so?"

"Oh, yeah. They're sneaky that way."

When she looked like she was going to start fussing with her hair—which was down around her shoulders and as pretty as ever—he leaned over and kissed her brow. "Come on. It's just dinner."

She got out of her side before he could get her door for her, but he let it slide. Instead, she looked like she was steeling herself to go into battle. Her chin was up, her shoulders were back and she looked determined to conquer the world. He could only hope that his parents wouldn't disappoint and that they'd be as great as he knew they could be.

Just as he helped her up the four steps leading to the landing by the front door, it swung open. And there were his parents, dressed casually—for them. His father was in jeans, loafers and a button-down. His mom was wearing a loose sleeveless sheath dress made out of black linen.

He and Liana looked almost like carbon copies. He was wearing his favorite pair of worn khaki chinos, Birkenstocks and a black polo. Liana was wearing a pale yellow sundress and gold flip-flops.

He noticed Liana had taken stock of everyone's outfits, too, because she breathed a sigh of relief just as his parents stepped forward.

"Hi, guys. We're so glad you're here," Mom said. Smiling brightly at Liana, she held out her hand. "I'm Peggy and this is my husband, Richard."

"Liana Mann. Thank you for having me."

After Kent shook his dad's hand and kissed his mother's cheek while Liana shook hands with both his parents, he rested his hand on the small of Liana's back. She didn't pull away, which he was grateful for. He wanted her to know that he literally and figuratively had her back. He wasn't going to allow her to flounder for one minute during this dinner.

To his relief, his parents walked them right through the entryway, to the kitchen, and then out on to the backyard patio. The patio was made of red brick, had a fire pit and was surrounded by eight or ten elm and birch trees. The iron patio furniture had bright orange cushions and was comfortable and cozy.

"Do you like salmon, Liana?" his father asked.

"Yes. I mean, I haven't had it that much but I'm sure I'll like it."

"We grilled it on a cedar plank and drizzled it with teriyaki and lemons," his dad said. "Teriyaki sauce makes everything better, right?"

Liana's lips curved into a beautiful smile for the first time all day. "I've always thought so."

"Kent, come help me with the drinks," his mom said as she headed toward the kitchen. "Arnold Palmers okay with you, Liana?"

"Do you know what an Arnold Palmer is?" Dad asked. "It's lemonade and iced tea."

"I know all about them. I make about thirty of them a day at the diner where I work."

Dad smiled. "Oh yeah? Is that the drink of choice?"

"It is in the summer." Liana made a move to get up. "Would you like some help, Peggy?"

"Not at all. That's what sons are for. You sit down and relax."

After double-checking to see that Liana looked just fine, Kent followed his mother inside. "What do you need me to do? Get out the drinks or the glasses?"

"The tea and lemonade. I'll put ice in the glasses."

Just as he got out the two pitchers, his mom smiled. "She's darling, Kent. So wholesome-looking, too."

"What is that supposed to mean?" he asked as he continued to fill each glass with lemonade and tea.

"Not a thing. I guess I just had a different vision of her." She sent him a pointed look. "Plus, it's not like you're one to give great descriptions or much information at all, Mr. Privacy."

He supposed he deserved that. It wasn't like he was going to call his parents and tell them how fascinated he was with Liana. "Ready to take the drinks out?"

"Yep. You take the glasses. I'll take the appetizers."

He noticed then that she had the oven door open and was pulling out her favorite puff pastry appetizers. Glad that she wasn't serving anything too crazy, he walked outside to join his dad and Liana. They were chatting together like they were best friends.

"I have drinks," he announced. "Mom's behind me with those puff pastry things she had in the freezer."

"We're going all out for you, girl," his dad teased. "Sunday appetizers aren't our norm."

Looking even more at ease, she smiled up at him. "I'm feeling more special by the minute."

"If this keeps up, I'm going to bring you here every Sunday, Liana," Kent said as he handed her a glass and then took a seat next to her. "Last weekend we ate hot dogs and tater tots."

"If I get to come again one day, I'll bring a dish."

"Anytime you want to join us, just show up," Mom said as she sat down. "Even if Kent can't make it."

He pretended to look affronted. "Wow. Thanks, Mom."

"Oh, you know what I meant," his mother said. "Help yourself, Liana."

And so it continued. Kent leaned back, sipped his drink and watched Liana come out of her shell. He'd never been so proud of his parents. They had somehow managed to make her feel special but like an old friend at the same time.

Later, when the fish and baked potatoes and greens were ready, they moved to the dining room. By this time Liana looked so relaxed, Kent figured she wouldn't have been nervous about anything they could have served.

The only uncomfortable bit came at the end when they were saying their goodbyes.

"I don't want you to leave without mentioning that we know Kent is working on your husband's case," his dad said. "I didn't work on it all those years ago but I was aware that it was never closed. I'm sorry about what you've been going through."

And just like that, Liana froze. Seeing that she'd paled slightly, Kent moved closer to her. "Dad, now's not the time."

Liana put one slim hand on his forearm. "Kent, it's okay." Turning to his father, she nodded. "Thank you for saying that."

"Kent's a good cop. He'll figure out what happened. I have no doubt about it."

But instead of looking pleased, a new shadow entered her eyes. "I guess we'll see what happens. I'm starting to realize that ten years really is a long time ago."

"Dad, I'm sorry, but we really do have to go," he said. No way did he want his father to start discussing old cases.

After flicking a glance at him, his dad nodded. "Right. Good to see you, son. And Liana, I hope to see you again soon."

His mother hugged her. "You're a delight, dear. Keep my boy in line."

"I'll do my best."

"I'll call you soon, Mom. Thanks."

His mother smiled. "Anytime, son."

When they got back to the car, he helped Liana in and then got in the driver's seat. As he pressed the button on his ignition, he exhaled deeply. "We survived."

When Liana giggled and smiled at him softly, he knew right then and there that they'd done more than that.

Chapter Twenty

Liana had been a nervous wreck the entire day, sure that the dinner with Kent's parents was going to be awful. By now she knew that Kent was well-spoken, well educated and came from parents who only wanted the best for him.

There wasn't a lot about her background that was the same. So she'd been worried about what they were going to ask her and how she was going to respond.

Among other things.

But she'd fallen in love with Richard and Peggy. She'd loved her parents, but they hadn't been around much. Then her mother had gotten sick and her father had just been plain tired. He'd been more of the kind of guy to sit in his chair by the TV and doze until she informed him that supper was ready.

But even when things had been pretty good, neither had been the type to joke around with her and her friends or to go all out for a Sunday dinner. They hadn't even done those things for Mason, which Liana figured said a lot. She'd never needed a counselor to explain why she'd gotten in a relationship with Billy

"And you want…what?" She really needed everything to be spelled out.

"I want to do something that actually shows you how serious I'm becoming about the two of us. Having you over at my parents' is a good first step."

"I guess it is."

"So what do you think?"

She thought she wanted the same thing he did. "I think I'm flattered by your invitation and I'm wondering what they'll think of me."

"Don't worry about that." Sounding confident again, Kent said, "Liana, they're going to love you. I promise they're not the type to ask you a dozen inappropriate questions, either. They're nice people."

He was making it sound like his parents were practically the Waltons. "Kent, your father is a cop, right? And your mother is a lawyer?"

"Yes." He paused. "Is something wrong with that?"

"Only that they don't quite sound like the easygoing, down-to-earth folks you're making them out to be. What do you think they're going to say when they discover we met because of one of your cold cases?"

"After getting to know you, my dad is going to say that I've never been too smart but that I've obviously been getting smarter in spite of myself. And my mother is going to say something just like that but using bigger words," he joked. "Please say yes, Liana."

"What Sunday are we talking about?"

"This Sunday."

"The day after tomorrow." Yes, she was sounding panicked.

"Yep. So what do you think?"

"Kent, I think that you've given me no notice and that I have to work tomorrow."

"This is for dinner, Li. What are you getting at?"

"I'm not going to have time to go shopping."

"Just wear whatever," he said like a guy who had never stared blankly at a closet full of clothes. "So it's a yes?"

"Yes." She couldn't believe she was agreeing so easily, but she didn't want to let him down. Or maybe it was herself she didn't want to let down.

"Great. I'll pick you up at five, Liana."

"I'll be ready." She didn't know how she was going to do it, but she would. Just as she was about to tell him that she was looking forward to it, she yawned. Almost immediately, he yawned, as well. "I guess we finally got tired."

"I guess so. Sleep well, Liana. Good night."

"You, too," she said softly before hanging up, throwing the last of the cake away and then trotting off to bed.

Hmm. It seemed she hadn't needed a chocolate fix after all. Just a good phone call with Kent Olson.

Mann. Liana knew—she'd never thought she deserved anyone better.

So Peggy and Richard Olson were amazing.

But they couldn't hold a candle to Kent. He'd been close to a hero in a TV movie that evening. The stuff that teenage girls' dreams were made of, before they realized that such dreams were never going to come true.

But maybe she'd been wrong.

After all, he'd been attentive and sweet from the time he picked her up to now, driving her home. He'd gone out of his way to make sure she was happy and didn't feel threatened. He waited on her. Encouraged her and held her hand. He'd even gently reminded his parents that they needed to keep things light with her, too.

He was still being sweet now, since he was driving her home and she hadn't done much besides gaze out the window and replay the whole surprising evening in her head.

When he slowed to take her exit off the highway, he glanced her way. "Did my parents wear you out so much that you need a nap? Are you exhausted?"

She smiled. "Pretty much. I mean, there's only so much fish, lemonade and strawberry shortcake a woman can take."

He reached for her hand and linked their fingers together. "That strawberry shortcake was really good. It's one of my mom's twelve things she can make," he teased.

"It was so good, I wouldn't care if she could make eleven other things or not. I'm going to tell Gabe to make it next time he gets a deal on strawberries."

"Seriously, I'm glad you came. I know my parents loved you."

"I loved them." Realizing how she sounded, she quickly added, "I mean, I'm sure everyone does."

His thumb ran across her knuckles, warming her, even though she hadn't thought she was cold. "I don't know if they do or not. All I cared about was that you looked happy."

She needed to be honest. "I was. Being with them and you, well, it made me feel like I was part of a real family. It was nice."

"I thought you were close to your brother and his family. No?"

She shrugged, hating where his mind was drifting, and hating that as much as she liked Kent, she couldn't trust him with her deepest fears about Mason. "I am. We drifted apart after my mother died but got close again after Dad passed on and he married Jeanie." And then talked less after Billy went missing.

"I'm sorry about that. I'm an only child, but I've heard that it's hard for siblings when both of their parents are gone."

She swallowed, knowing that wasn't the whole reason for their distance. "I think you're right." When he glanced at her again, Liana knew that she needed to say something more. "Losing both of our parents has made us feel adrift, but some of our distance is simply logistics. He's busy with his job and family and I'm busy with my job and my artwork."

"Does he have a child?"

"One. A little boy who's five. Cooper is in kindergarten and playing soccer and T-ball. They're busy." That was true, too. It just wasn't the whole truth about why she and Mason were no longer close.

"Hey, I want you to know that my parents meant what they said. They'd love to see you again."

Realizing they were almost at her house, Liana knew it was time to go back to reality. "And you?"

He looked surprised. "Me? You know I want to see you again."

"I mean, do you want me to see your parents again?"

"Liana, of course."

Though it was tempting to simply smile, she knew that she needed to remind them both of why they'd met in the first place. "Even if the case never gets settled?" Or if he found out something that might change his mind about her?

"What are you talking about? Liana, I meant what I said the other night. I'm serious about you. I'm fine with taking everything slow—but what you and I are discovering is special. It doesn't have anything to do with my job."

She wasn't sure about that. "If you change your mind, let me know, okay?"

He chuckled like she was being ridiculous. "I will, but you don't have anything to worry about. As much as I'd like to solve this case and get out of the basement, I'm working hard to sort out Billy's death for you, too, Li."

"Me?"

"Of course. I want you to be able to sleep at night without worrying that whoever attacked him is going to attack you."

The words were hard to hear because she knew how wrong Kent had it. She'd been worried about Billy coming back, maybe even taking his revenge out on her. Never about getting attacked.

"Thank you for worrying about me."

They were in her driveway. His headlights cast twin beams on her garage door. Their light, combined with the lights she always left burning by her front door, illuminated his expression. "I want to worry about you. I like it." Squeezing her hand once more, he said, "Wait here. I want to get your door."

She sat tight and let him walk around, then help her out. "Keys?"

She held up her purse. "Right here."

"Get them out and I'll help you inside, 'kay?"

He was being bossy but she knew he wasn't trying to control her, just keep her safe. And, because she wouldn't mind not walking into an empty house after dark for once, she got out her keys, then handed them to him when he held out his hand. After unlocking her door, he turned on her entryway light and glanced around.

"Want me to do a walkthrough, just to make sure you're safe?"

"No. I'm fine."

"All right." He reached for her hands. For the first time since she'd known him, he looked almost unsure. "Liana, when I told you that my parents loved you, I didn't tell you something else. Something a lot more important."

"What's that?"

"That they aren't the only ones who are falling in love."

Her heart expanded. Honestly, she thought her whole body had turned to mush. But she still wasn't ready to say those words back to him. Not yet. "You say the sweetest things."

His smile faltered. "You aren't sure yet?"

"Don't you remember that we're supposed to be taking things slowly?"

"I haven't forgotten." Leaning down, he kissed her on the forehead. "I'll give you all the time you need. I've got nothing but time."

She might need time, but there was no way she was going to let him just kiss her on the forehead like Liana was his little sister. "I could be wrong, but I'm pretty sure that even people who are still figuring things out can kiss good-night."

"I was hoping you'd say that."

Kent pulled her toward him. When their lips touched, she closed her eyes and wrapped her arms around his neck. It had been so, so long since she'd been kissed so tenderly. So long since she'd even been interested in kissing another man. But with Kent, everything felt so fresh and new. Untainted by all the bad that had been in her marriage.

As Liana sought his comfort, she thought about two things. She didn't just *think* she was falling in love, she was pretty sure.

The second? When he found out that she was withholding information from him—and that it might cost him everything—he was never going to forgive her.

Everything that they'd built would come tumbling down and he would vanish, just like Billy had all those years ago. And then all she would have were another set of memories that she wished were better than they actually were.

Chapter Twenty-One

Kent hated to be questioning people around Adams County without telling Liana that he was nearby, but it couldn't be helped. He needed to get some information, and he needed to get it without Liana either preventing people from speaking or swaying his decisions and choices. Not that he thought she would…but if he was wrong, it would jeopardize this case and he couldn't allow anything to do that.

But even though his intentions were good, Kent was starting to wonder if he was ever going to be able to do anything without thinking about Liana Mann first.

It was official. He was a goner where she was concerned. No doubt about it.

The only thing standing in their way was this case. Even though their relationship didn't depend on his success, his failure could make things a lot harder for them. Kent feared that if she never got closure with her husband's death, it would always haunt her.

He didn't mind her being hesitant to commit to him. He actually didn't even blame her. How could she move forward with so many unanswered questions in her past?

That was why, after rereading Officer Grune's careful notes, he took a chance and visited a resale shop on the edge of Peebles. The store was large and well organized, and the shop's owner obviously took a lot of time to care for the store's appearance and upkeep. It was bright and cheery inside, and had a good number of customers in it, even though it was barely ten in the morning.

Within five minutes of entering, a well-dressed woman in her mid-to-late-fifties walked up. "Hey there," she said with a friendly smile. "Something I can help you with?"

"I hope so. I'm looking for Janice Rodina. Any chance you're her?"

"I am." Pale green eyes looked him over. "Who might you be?"

"I'm Officer Olson. Kent, ma'am." He held out a card and flashed his badge. "I'd like to speak to you for a few minutes."

She didn't budge. "What's going on?"

"I have reason to believe that you might be familiar with the case I'm working on."

Her eyes widened but she didn't show any other reaction. "I guess we'd better go visit in my office. Hold on a sec."

He watched her speak to the pair of women behind the counter, grab her cell phone, then turn back to him. "Follow me on back, Officer."

Her office looked like any other back office of a retail manager's. Besides a desk and chair, the space was filled with metal shelves containing excess merchandise, sales tickets, tags, markers and a metal lock box. A fold-up card table on the other side of the room was obviously the employees' lunch space and coffee bar.

Watching him scan the area, she said, "I would apologize for the mess, but it actually looks pretty good in here today."

"Nothing to apologize for. I appreciate your time." He pulled out a pad of paper and a pen. "I hope I won't take up too much of it."

She gestured to the two metal chairs next to the folding table. "Have a seat, and don't worry about my time. We had a violent woman in here about a year ago. She wandered in and asked to use the bathroom, and when we told her no, she proceeded to throw a fit. The cops got here in less than ten minutes and saved the day. I'm still grateful."

"Glad we could help."

"Me, too." She crossed her legs. "So how can I help you?"

"I'm working on an unsolved case from ten years ago. A man went missing, practically without a trace."

"Oh? What was his name?"

"Billy Mann. Did you know him?"

She hesitated. "I think a lot of people knew him, Officer."

"What do you remember about Billy?"

"What do I remember?" She blew out a breath of air. It caused her bangs to flutter slightly on her forehead. "Well, let's see. He was loud and had a great smile."

"Anything else?"

"Sure I do. Off the top of my head, I'd say Billy Mann was a real jerk, and I'm only using that particular word because you're a cop and I don't want to tick you off."

He smiled. "I appreciate that, but feel free to use whatever words you want to describe him."

"Let me put it this way. Billy was the kind of guy you might run into at the convenience store. He might catch your attention because he was cursing at the soda machine or because they didn't have the chips he wanted or because there were too many people in line or because the sky was still blue. So your first impression might be to give him a wide berth because it was obvious that he was strung kinda tight." Janice glanced at him. When he nodded, she continued. "After that, maybe you'd give Billy a second look because he had a good smile on him."

She folded her hands on her knee. "But then, after you get that second look, you try to stay clear of him. Because he wasn't reasonable, you know? Like, the soda machine worked just fine, the store never had the chips he was looking for, there were only two people in line, and no matter how much he ranted and complained, the sky never had been green."

"So he made up things to fuss about."

Her gaze hardened. "No, Officer. He made up things to get crazy about." She leaned back and folded her hands together. "There's a difference, right?"

"Right."

After another pause, she muttered, "I never understood why his wife stayed with him."

"So you knew he was married."

"Of course I did," Janice said. "Everyone around here knew that Liana only married Billy Mann because her father encouraged it. Adams County's a fairly good size, but we're all real small-town."

"Did you ever talk to Liana about her husband?"

She looked surprised that he'd asked. "Of course not."

"Why didn't you?"

"I didn't because no matter how bad I thought her husband is, a woman doesn't say any of that to the wife. Marriage is tough enough without other people stepping in where they don't belong."

He kept his expression carefully blank. "I see."

"That doesn't mean I don't regret that, though," she blurted.

"Why is that?"

Janice looked away as she replied. "One day Liana came in here with about a pound of makeup on her face. She was moving slow, too. Said she'd fallen on a patch of ice on the driveway. But she wasn't fooling anyone. We all knew Billy had beaten her up bad." Still looking haunted by the memory, she murmured, "I was tempted to call the cops right then and there."

It was incredibly hard to not react to her words. Kent hated the thought of Liana being so hurt and no one ever wanting to step in. "Why didn't you?" he asked before he could stop himself. "Because it wasn't your business?"

Janice lifted her chin. "No, sir. I didn't call the cops because when Liana and I were talking about the cold weather, she mentioned something about her brother stopping by her house and getting so mad at her appearance that he drove off in a hurry. That was good enough for me."

"What was good enough, Janice?"

"Come on, Officer. We both know what she meant."
The woman's striking green eyes sharpened. "I figured
Liana's kin was going to look after her."

"What day was that? Do you remember?"

She shrugged. "It was a long time ago."

"I realize that," he said impatiently. "But all I'm looking for is an idea of time. Was it a couple of days or a
week before Billy Mann went missing? After?"

Janice pursed her lips. "I don't remember the exact
date, but I do remember that it was the day Billy Mann
went missing."

He went cold. "Are you sure about that?"

"Oh, yeah." She paused a moment, then added, "I remember thinking that Mason likely caught up with old
Billy. Uh, not that I ever knew that for sure."

"Did you call the cops about your suspicions?"

"Of course not. I never said nothing to anyone about
it." Her tone was almost belligerent. "And before you
act all surprised, you've got to try to see things from
the outside."

"Which was?"

"That I was glad Billy Mann was out of Liana's life.
I don't hold with a man beating up his wife. Say what
you want about a person's rights and such, but it ain't
right. As far as Liana was concerned, I thought she was
better off without him." Janice looked at Kent steadily.
"Anyone would've been better off without him."

She stood up and folded her arms across her chest.
"And don't you go telling me that the cops would've
done all kinds of good, either. You and I both know
that some dumb-as-rocks patrolman could've gone out
to Liana's house and made things worse."

He didn't know if that would've happened or not. All

he did know was that if he hadn't sworn to uphold the law, he might have felt the same way Janice did.

Now all he did know was that he was going to have to go talk to Mason, and he was dreading the conversation already.

Chapter Twenty-Two

"Liana, you've got company," Angel announced as she walked into the vast commercial kitchen of Dig In Diner.

Liana looked up from her spot at the small table in the back corner of the room. Gabe had made her a burger and she'd opted to eat it in his company instead of sitting by herself in the small break room.

"Who is it?" she asked.

"Who do you think?" Angel quipped as she chomped a fresh piece of gum. "Mr. tall, dark and detective."

"How does he look?"

"Fine."

Ignoring both Angel's saucy smile and Gabe's chuckle, Liana said, "I meant, does he look happy? Upset?"

"Hmm. I don't know…maybe anxious to see you?"

Gabe looked at the clock above the door leading to the dining room. "You might as well clock out now, Liana. It's dead in here and you're only on for another two hours, anyway."

"Do you mind closing, Angel?" Liana asked. Leaving early to spend time with Kent sounded wonderful, but not if it put her girlfriend in a bind.

"Nope. I need the hours. Go on."

"All right. Will you tell Kent that I'll be right out?"

"Sure thing." She was out of the kitchen in a flash.

Gabe playfully winced. "You're a brave woman, Liana Mann. There's no telling what Angel is going to find time to tell Kent before you get to him."

"You're right." Frowning, she wrapped up the other half of her burger to take with her.

"You aren't going to take that with you, are you?"

"Of course I am. You make a great cheeseburger, Gabe." Plus, some old habits were hard to break. Even though she didn't have money problems anymore, it was hard not to let good food go to waste.

Gabe waved her compliment off. "I'll make you another one anytime. It's just half a burger, child. Besides, it's only six. I'd wager that your man has shown up to try to take you out to eat, anyway."

After hesitating for another few seconds, Liana did as Gabe suggested and tossed the last of it into the trash, rushed to the washroom to get off some of the diner smell, pulled her purse out of her locker, then walked out to the dining room.

Kent was sitting on one of the bar stools at the counter, sipping coffee and chatting with Viv. When he caught sight of her, he got to his feet. "Hey, that was quick," he said.

"I figured I'd best hurry before Angel talked your ear off."

He grinned. "Just as she was settling in to ask me twenty questions, two sets of folks walked through the door. Viv put her to work."

"Do you need to give her a hand?" Kent asked her. "If you want, we can talk during your next break."

"No need for that." Feeling a little giddy, she beamed at him. "Guess what? I can leave. Gabe let me clock out early."

But instead of looking delighted, Kent seemed taken aback. "Oh? Well, that's great, but I...well, I still have some work to do, I'm afraid."

She realized then that his badge was on display on his belt and he had on his work uniform—a black polo shirt, dark khakis with a solid crease on the legs and thick-soled brown loafers. His clothes, together with his reserved manner, told her that he hadn't come to see her because he couldn't stand to be away from her for another minute.

Realizing that he must have only stopped by to bring some news about the case, she swallowed her disappointment. "Would you like to go outside to talk?" Liana asked.

"Sure."

When Kent made a move to pay for his coffee, Viv stopped him. "Save your money. Coffee's always on the house for cops. You know that."

"See you in two days, Viv," Liana said as they headed toward the door.

"Enjoy your time off. Don't work too hard."

After waving goodbye to Angel, too, Liana walked through the door that Kent was holding open for her. "Where would you like to talk?" she asked. "I would say we could sit over at the picnic table, but you look kind of serious."

"Do you mind if we talk in your car?"

This had to be serious, since he never willingly suggested her vehicle. "Not at all." She pulled out her key fob and clicked the button that unlocked it.

He got in the passenger seat and kept his attention straight ahead as she got situated on her side. Things were getting weirder and weirder.

She was tempted to ask him what was going on but she decided to simply wait for him to gather his thoughts.

"Liana, I've been racking my brain, trying to think of a good way to tell you this. But here's the thing. I don't think there is a good way."

"You're scaring me, Kent. What is wrong? Are you sick?" Was he breaking up with her?

"Oh no. It's nothing like that," he said quickly. "It has to do with the case."

So her suspicions were right. "Okay…"

"I'm about to go speak to your brother."

"What do you need to talk to Mason about?" she asked. Hearing her voice, Liana knew she sounded confused, but that wasn't the complete truth. She actually had a pretty good idea why Kent needed to speak with her brother. She hadn't ever thought it would happen, but it looked like everything was coming out in the open after all.

Looking torn, Kent frowned. "Liana, I'm sorry, and I know I've been asking you for help, but I can't speak to you about my reasons. I just didn't want you to hear about this from someone besides me."

"Hear about what? You aren't telling me anything." Inwardly, she winced. She sounded hurt and defensive, which wasn't fair to him at all.

"Hopefully you'll know soon enough."

Kent sounded so cryptic, she was starting to feel a

little angry. It was almost like he was playing a game with her. "You're acting like Mason is a suspect." When he simply stared at her, she realized that was exactly what he was. "That's it. You do think he killed Billy."

"Do you want to tell me why you think he could be considered one?"

His voice was smooth and sounded just like Officer Grune's tone when she was questioning her those first days after Billy's disappearance. She hated that he was talking to her that way. "Who have you been talking to?" she asked. "What have people been saying? Don't forget, all this happened a long time ago."

"I haven't forgotten, Liana." His voice was low and gravelly. "And you know I can't tell you what I've heard."

Though her head was telling her that he was trying to be sympathetic to what she was going through, all she felt was pain. She folded her arms over her chest, not even caring that it looked like she was trying to protect herself. Maybe that was what she was doing, anyway. "Is there anything else you want to say?"

"There is. I'd like you to tell me more about your daily life with Billy in the days before he died." When she just stared at him, his expression went blank. "If you could do that, I'd appreciate it."

She hated this conversation. Hated that she'd been imagining that Kent stopped by because he'd missed her. Hated that she'd put on lipstick and washed up because she thought he wanted to take her out.

Hated that she was becoming disappointed yet again. Looking straight ahead, she thought back ten years and gave Kent what he needed to hear. "I didn't have a real big *daily life* with him. The last year of our marriage,

Billy went down a dark spiral. He went from being indifferent to me, to being angry all the time, to addicted to too many substances to count. I went from trying to save our marriage to trying to make him happy to avoiding him as much as I could. That's how things were."

"You've told me before that he hurt you."

"You're right, I did." Feeling angry that she had to relive the abuse yet again, she added, "But hurt is a pretty vague description, isn't it?" She glanced his way.

Still looking stoic, Kent nodded.

Liana mentally rolled her eyes. "How about if I say that he beat me? Is that clear enough? What about if I tell you that the last six months of our marriage, he abused me in multiple ways and that I was in constant pain. Does that help your case?" she asked sarcastically.

"Did Mason know about that?"

"He suspected." Actually, Mason had known for a fact. Especially the day that he'd stopped by the house.

Kent sighed. "Liana, I think you're still keeping things from me."

"Still?" she asked warily.

"I care about you. A lot. But I also want to do my job. I have to do it. It's not an option, Liana."

"I know that. Of course I know that."

"If you do, then you must know that you could have saved me a lot of time by being much more forthcoming."

He might have a job to do, but she had been the one getting hurt. Back then she'd felt completely alone. She would've never sought help—she'd been too afraid of what Billy would do to her. But when Mason had stopped by and been so upset on her behalf, she'd at last felt a burst of hope.

But since Kent had probably never felt that way, she knew he wouldn't understand. "What are you going to say to Mason?" she asked at last.

Kent looked even more disappointed in her. "I debated coming over here first. I knew I shouldn't but I couldn't leave you in the dark. Not when you've already been through so much. But so help me, Liana, if you get on the phone right now and call or text him that I'm driving out to see him, I'm going to have a hard time forgiving you."

"This is my garbage that you're asking him about. Mine. You can't blame him for worrying about me."

"Don't call him, Li." He leveled a hard look at her. "If you do, I'll know."

Before she could say another word, he got out of the car, closed the door behind him and walked to his own. Minutes later he was out of sight.

Sitting there all alone, she was torn. If she didn't warn Mason that Kent was on his way, then her brother would say she was choosing her boyfriend over him. But if she did tell Mason, Liana knew without a doubt that she would lose everything she'd gained with Kent.

Plus, there was a very good chance that even if she did tell Mason, it wouldn't change the outcome of what was going to happen.

That was one thing Liana was very sure about. No matter what, as soon as Mason admitted to killing Billy, she was going to lose a piece of herself that she could never get back again.

But maybe she'd already lost it, anyway.

Chapter Twenty-Three

Kent pulled over into an empty shopping center plaza less than a mile from the Dig In Diner. So many emotions were rushing through him, he knew he had to get a handle on himself before he met his father in a grocery store parking lot about a mile from where Mason was working at a tire and auto part retailer.

Putting his vehicle into Park, he shut off the engine and simply leaned his head back against his seat.

"What did you expect?" he said out loud to himself. "Liana was a battered wife with little to no support system. Her parents had taught her not to expect too much from other people, and then the cops who handled her case let her down. Of course she's going to be guarded around you."

Thinking about Doug Evans, the lead detective on the case, and Officer Grune's notes that had been compiled about Billy's disappearance, Kent knew that Liana hadn't received much help at all. Actually, she'd been thought to be a suspect until her alibi checked out.

Then, after hearing next to nothing for ten years, a team of officers informed her that her husband's body had been found. Even though she would've guessed that would happen, it had to have been quite a shock. And now here he was, dredging up painful memories all over again—because he was hoping to resurrect his career.

So of course Liana had trust issues, both in her personal life and with the police. But less than thirty minutes ago, when he'd been trying to talk to her about Mason, Kent realized that she hadn't been shocked about Mason being a suspect. Seconds after that he'd had to face the hard truth—that all this time, Liana had been fairly sure that her brother was responsible for her husband's death—or at least for his disappearance.

But she'd never said a word to him.

Even after he told her he was falling for her. Even after they'd shared that kiss. He felt betrayed and hurt. Like he'd done so much work for nothing.

It was probably the way the other cops had felt about his arrogance affecting their case. Maybe Liana's behavior was nothing less than he deserved.

When the chime of his cell phone pulled him out of his thoughts, he answered it in relief. "Hey, Dad."

"Kent, sorry, but I'm another ten minutes out. I got hung up in a never-ending meeting with the commissioner. If you want to go ahead without me, I understand."

He didn't trust himself to handle things on his own, which was hard to admit. After everything he'd been through, he was still too weak to do a decent job on his own. "That's no problem. I don't mind waiting."

"Are you sure? Hey, did something happen? You don't sound like yourself."

"Something happened, but I'll tell you about it later. I'm fine."

"Still want to meet near the IPA?"

He stared up at the grocery store's sign he was already parked in front of. "Yep. Take your time, Dad."

After they disconnected, he got out of his car and leaned against it. He had to get a handle on himself. Breathing hard, he felt the warm metal sink through his shirt, heating his skin. Then, at last, he focused.

He was standing in a dead shopping center. At one time a K-Mart or Sears or some retailer had been the focal point of it. Presumably, when that store closed, the other shops nearby—the ones that had depended on the large retailer to bring in the people—had closed up, too.

Now it looked like there was no reason for the public to be in the parking lot at all. There was nothing beyond a handful of for-lease signs and a couple of cars with for-sale signs on their windows.

It wasn't anything that everyone in the community hadn't seen before all over the city. The financial collapse and recession had been hard in Ohio. Especially small, rural areas like Adams County that hadn't been generating a lot of income in the first place.

Of course, things were better here now. At least until the next financial battle played out across the heartland. It was sad, really.

Then, in the corner, he spied a small sign. Curious, he walked to it and saw neat handwriting. Coming Soon! Millie's Coffee and Pies! Underneath the words was the outline of an Amish buggy and horse.

Huh. It looked like someone was ignoring the dozen reasons why this place wasn't a desirable spot to start a new business.

Hope sprang eternal.

Hope.

To his surprise, a verse from Psalm 42 filled his heart.

Why am I discouraged? Why is my heart so sad? I will put my hope in God! I will praise him again—my Savior and my God!

He hadn't thought about that verse in years. It had been his Sunday school teacher's favorite verse. Mrs. Johnson had quoted it at least once a month. So much so that he had rolled his eyes at her recital more than once.

But now, as he thought about his insecurities and his failures, he realized that all this time, Mrs. Johnson had been right. He'd needed to stop looking for the worst in himself and expecting the worst to happen and start having hope and faith in the Lord. Just like Millie and her upcoming coffee shop, it seemed.

He closed his eyes and said a quick prayer of thanks. He wasn't sure about everything that the Lord was trying to tell him, but he knew that if it was as simple as to have hope in himself, in the process and in Liana, it was enough. Maybe more than enough.

Thirty minutes later Kent was sitting with his father in his dad's roomy SUV. He'd just filled him in on his conversation with Liana.

"I'm surprised you didn't go right over and confront Mason, Kent."

"I didn't trust myself to see him on my own."

His father raised his eyebrows. "Really? Has this whole transfer to cold cases really done such a number on you?"

"Yeah, my confidence has taken a beating, but it's more than that. Dad, I don't want to mess this up. Billy Mann was no prize but that doesn't mean his case doesn't deserve to be solved and the right person pay for the crime."

His father studied him for another long moment, then nodded. "Let's go pay Mason a visit."

When they arrived at the automotive shop, Kent was glad to see that it was almost empty. Two of the three bays were empty and there were only four cars in the parking lot.

After speaking into his radio, letting the station know where they were, Kent and his father alighted. Then, with his father steps behind, Kent entered the office.

A guy in his late forties who'd been looking at his phone popped his head up when the door closed behind them. "Can I help you?" he asked.

Kent showed his badge. "We're looking for Mason Kelly. He around?"

The guy got to his feet. "Yeah. He's in the back." After taking two or three steps toward the glass door that obviously led to the bays, he paused and turned back to them. "Is everything okay?"

"Yep," his father said in his usual relaxed way. "We're just following up on something...sorry, I didn't catch your name."

"Sorry, it's Don. Don Burke."

"This won't take long, Don," his father murmured. "Just routine."

"Oh, sure." When he opened the door, they were surrounded by the mournful twang of a George Strait ballad. "Hey, Mason. You here?"

"Yeah! Finishing up this Pontiac now."

"Get Jesse to finish it up. Someone's here to see you."

While his father waited patiently, Kent headed toward the red Pontiac, walking by the open garage bay, just in case Mason had a mind to scoot out of there.

Thankfully, he didn't. Mason was looking curiously at the pair of them while carefully wiping oil off his hands. "You look like cops," he said.

His father grinned. "That's because we are cops." He held up his badge. "Richard Olson."

Kent joined them and flashed his badge, as well. "I'm Officer Kent Olson."

Mason's eyebrows rose. "Y'all related or something?"

"Richard's my dad."

"Keeping it all in the family?"

It looked like Mason was barely holding back a snarky comment. Kent guessed he probably couldn't blame him. "Where can we talk?"

"I'm due for a break. How about outside so I can smoke?"

Kent gestured for him to lead the way. Mason stepped off to the side, toward a beat-up plastic black trash can next to a pair of rusty metal chairs.

"Have a seat if you'd like," Mason said as he lit a Marlboro Red.

"Doubt one of those chairs would hold me," his dad said. "I'll stand."

Mason shrugged as he exhaled a plume of smoke. "Suit yourself. So what's up?"

"I wanted to speak to you about Billy Mann."

"Billy?"

"He was your brother-in-law, yes?"

"Yeah." His whole expression changed. "For four long years."

"Then he went missing."

Mason looked back at Kent. His eyes were the exact shade of his sister's but without any of the vulnerability that seemed to be so at home in Liana. "Yeah, he sure did. And you guys were no help." He took another drag before he added, "My poor sister had to deal with a bunch of questions and uncertainty for ten years. It just about killed her."

"Sounds like you were really concerned about Liana."

Mason's whole posture changed. "What do you want from me?" he asked, a new edge in his tone.

"I want you to think back ten years ago and remember when you stopped by Liana's house and saw that Billy had hurt her."

Mason tossed his cigarette butt on the ground and rubbed it out with the toe of his boot. "Hurt her? Is that what she said, or is it a cop's way of describing it?"

"Why don't you tell us what you saw?" his dad asked.

"I saw that my sister looked like crap. She had a black eye and could barely walk. And you know what that loser's excuse was?"

Still looking directly at Mason, Kent shook his head.

"He was mad because Liana had brought home too much money from the job she had back then. She used to look after an old lady who had dementia. She'd clean and cook for her. The kids gave her a bonus as a thank-you but Billy refused to believe it," Mason said. "He called her a liar even though anyone could've backed up her claim."

"That doesn't make much sense," Dad said.

"Of course it doesn't, but it didn't need to in the first place," Mason bit out. "None of us thought he was good enough for her when they married, but my parents were sure Billy would get better. That my little sister was somehow going to convince him to become a whole new person." His jaw tightened. "But he didn't change. Only got worse."

"What did you do when you saw your sister?"

Mason stiffened. "What do you mean?"

"Did you take her to the doctor?"

"No. She wouldn't go. She never would go." He fumbled in his pocket. Pulled out another cigarette but didn't light it.

"I have a statement from someone who says that as soon as you saw your sister, you took off to go find Billy," Kent said.

Mason blinked, then looked like he was trying not to smile. "Wait, is that what you've decided happened to him? I saw my sister beat up, so I ran after him and killed him so he wouldn't hurt her again?"

"Wouldn't be the first time a brother did something like that," his father murmured.

"Look, I did go find him. But he was with all his new friends." He waved a hand. "A bunch of losers. Drug dealers. He was already hopped up on something."

"Did you say anything to him?"

"No." Mason pursed his lips. "I probably should've, but I didn't trust those guys not to shoot me for getting in their business."

Kent didn't bother to hide his disbelief. "So you ran out to find Billy, but then you got scared of his friends and left? Just like that?"

"Yeah." His expression was perfectly blank. "That's the kind of great brother I was, Officers. My sister had herself an abusive, drug-addicted, drug-dealing husband and I didn't even so much as touch the guy. Just in case I might get hurt, too. So that's what I've had to live with."

"Not really," said his father quietly. "After all, by all accounts, no one ever saw your brother-in-law again."

Mason finally lit the cigarette that he'd been holding on to like a lifeline. "You're exactly right. It was like one minute he was in our lives and I couldn't get him out of it, and the next? He was gone."

"That had to be an answer to a prayer," Kent murmured.

"To a prayer?" Mason shrugged. "I don't know. Maybe it was." His voice grew calm, almost reflective. "I do know that I was pretty happy to see the last of him, if you want to know the truth."

"I'm surprised to hear you say that."

Mason gave him an incredulous look. "He beat my sister. Jeanie and I had been trying to convince Liana to leave him for months but she'd always refused." After taking another drag from his cigarette and exhaling, he added, "Weeks later Liana put on weight. Then she started painting, and got that job at the diner, and even began to smile for a while. She had ten years of happiness. And then you went and found him."

The statement hung in the air as Mason inhaled another dose of nicotine.

And when a thin cloud of smoke dissipated in the air, Kent realized he didn't have a single thing more to say.

Nothing that mattered, anyway.

Chapter Twenty-Four

The conversation with Mason had gone on for longer than Kent had anticipated. It had also been about ten times more productive than he'd imagined. After Mason took off, Kent reported in to Sergeant Crier while his father checked his phone for messages.

"What did you think about that guy?" his dad asked as they headed back to his vehicle. "I found him to be a surprise."

"I felt the same way. He was far more forthcoming and honest than I thought he'd be," Kent replied.

"Do you think he did it?"

Kent weighed his words carefully as they walked to his car. Though he knew his father wasn't setting him up or giving him some kind of verbal test, he did expect a thoughtful response. And the case deserved it, too. "Before we started talking to Mason, there was no question in my mind that he'd killed his brother-in-law. He had the motive and the means to do it. But now…" His voice drifted off.

"Now you aren't so sure?"

He looked up at his father and saw a professional

curiosity in his eyes. He wasn't just going through the motions and waiting for Kent to keep up. "No, sir. I'm not. Honestly, I'm not sure about anything right now."

Thinking back on the conversation, even on the way Mason had stood there, smoking that one cigarette and trying so hard not to have a second, it had seemed that the guy hadn't had a thing to hide. "I thought he would've acted like he was guilty."

"He still holds a lot of anger for Billy. I guess I can't blame him."

"I can't blame him, either." Hating that he felt like a rookie instead of a cop who'd been on the force for years, Kent added, "I don't know what I thought I would discover during our conversation, Dad. I guess I thought he would have acted more paranoid or shifty or something? I've interviewed a lot of suspects, and I could be wrong—but I was starting to think that I had a good feel for hearing the truth."

"I was feeling the same things you were, Kent."

"Really? What made you rethink your perception of him?"

"The way he was so disgusted with the police. It was like he had given up on us doing anything to help his sister, locate his brother-in-law or now find the killer." Flicking on the turn signal, he entered the empty parking lot where Kent's sedan was waiting. "If he'd had more to do with Billy's death, I don't think he would've been quite so gutsy."

"Unless he's a psychopath."

"If he was, he probably would've killed someone else by now," Dad pointed out. "Do you think that's a possibility?"

"Nope." Unbuckling his seat belt, he said, "So Mason

Kelly looks to be a dead end. Where do you think that leaves me now?"

"You? What happened to *us*?" He raised an eyebrow. "Are you getting rid of me as your sidekick already?"

"Of course not. But you have your own caseload. Besides... I should probably solve this on my own for Sergeant Crier." And for his reputation. No one was going to give him the time of day at the station house if it became widely known that he'd had to get his father's help to solve a cold case.

"I wouldn't fret much about Crier's opinion of you. The guy's been around the block a few times."

"At least," Kent said in a dry tone.

"He's a good cop and always has been. The thing about Crier is that he's down in cold-case world because that's where he chooses to be. He gives those cases—and the people who are suffering because they remain unsolved—the dignity they deserve."

Immediately, Kent tried to backtrack. "Sorry. I didn't mean to make it sound like Sergeant Crier didn't know what he was doing. I completely respect him."

"Kent, you're forgetting something. There's a reason this case wasn't solved the first time around. It wasn't poor policing skills. It's the fact that it's plain confounding."

"I'll look over my notes from today and go back over the file again. I feel like I've missed something that's staring me right in the face."

"If you want me to reach out to my contacts again, I will," his father offered.

"Thank you, but my gut says Joe and his crew didn't have anything to do with Billy's death. I just didn't think they cared enough for him to kill him and then cart his body out to the state park."

"I'm inclined to agree. The broken neck and the gunshot wound, combined with the cuffs on his wrists seems personal." With a grimace he added, "Yeah. It was personal. Very personal."

"Thanks again for coming. I really appreciate it."

"It wasn't a problem at all. Actually, I think it did me good to get out of the office for a while. Sometimes I think all I ever do anymore is paperwork." Placing the vehicle in Park, he said, "Switching topics…should I tell your mother that you'll see her at church on Sunday?"

"Yep. I'll be there for Sunday supper, too."

"You going to bring Liana again?" There was a note of hope in his voice even as he held up a hand. "I'm just asking for your mother."

Hating that he was going to have to disappoint them both, he looked away. "I'll see, but I kind of doubt it, Dad."

"Supper with us was too tough, huh?"

"Not at all. Liana told me that she really liked y'all and I believe her. It's more that I told her we were going to pay a call on her brother today. She didn't seem too pleased about that."

His father chuckled. "Families. No matter what, they're the ties that bind, right?"

"Right." Kent clasped his dad's forearm for a moment before getting out and heading to his vehicle. But as his father drove off and he got into his own car, there was something about his father's parting words that resonated with him.

Families. Ties that bind. Personal. Boy, could it really be that simple? And if it was, would Liana ever forgive him for what he was about to do?

Wanting, no *needing*, to connect with her again, he quickly punched in her number. While it rang, he ran through a number of things he could say. Some were short and to the point, while others were more drawn out and heartfelt.

"Hello, this is Liana—"

"Liana, this is Kent," he began, before stopping abruptly. He'd gotten her recorded message, not her.

She hadn't picked up.

Disconnecting the call, he tossed his phone on the seat next to him and tried to remind himself that there were a number of possible reasons she hadn't answered. The most likely was that she was painting and therefore ignoring everything else.

But a sixth sense—or maybe it was just his heart— was telling him the most likely scenario. She hadn't picked up his call on purpose.

Because he had nothing else to say that she wanted to hear.

Chapter Twenty-Five

She didn't often paint late at night after working an eight-hour shift at the diner, but Liana couldn't resist. Ever since Kent had asked why she was still working at the diner when she obviously didn't need the paycheck, the hours spent there had felt tedious.

Oh, it wasn't that she didn't enjoy Angel, Viv, Gabe and the other people she worked with—or her customers. It was that the thought of spending every day with her art simply sounded so good. Now, every time she served a grumpy tourist or fended off a flirt or felt a twinge in her lower back when she mopped the floors at night, Liana was reminded that she didn't have to do it anymore.

The moment she'd gone home, she'd taken a long shower and slipped on her favorite old jeans and painting shirt. Then, after taking a cursory look at her mail, she'd turned on the radio to an oldies station and retreated to her studio.

Before long, the scent of her oils, combined with the joy she received from doing an activity she loved, revived her. She turned the music up a little louder, let her mind drift a little more and was soon consumed by her latest canvas.

The chime of her doorbell followed by incessant knocking pulled her away with a start.

"Hold on, I'm coming!" she called out as she picked up a rag and wiped down her brushes before rushing to the door. For the first time in ages, she pulled it open without looking. Maybe Martha or Sol was sick or had an emergency?

But the moment she faced the person on the other side, she wished she'd taken a moment to peek out the window first, if only to give her a second to conceal her shock.

"Mason, what are you doing here?"

He smirked as he gestured to her right hand. She was still holding two paintbrushes. "Guess I now know why you didn't answer the first two times I rang the bell."

"Sorry. I had the music up loud…"

"I know you get in your own world. Turn it down though, yeah? I don't know if I can handle hearing 'yackety yak, don't talk back' another second."

"Sorry." She rushed to the kitchen and turned off the Bluetooth device. Then, with her back still toward him, she attempted to get a grip. "Would you like something to drink?" she called out.

He joined her. "Got a beer in that fridge, by chance?"

"Not a one. You know I don't drink."

"I know. Thought maybe you had something every now and then, though."

"Nope." She opened the refrigerator. "How about a root beer? It's cold."

"Yeah, pour me a cold one, Li."

She got out two cold bottles and twisted the caps before handing him one. "Want to sit down?"

He took a sip from his bottle. "Sure." He led the way to her living room. Not that she would have taken him any place else, but it wasn't lost on Liana that she was following his lead, just like she always had. Even after all this time and everything she'd been through, Liana reckoned there would always be a part of her that would look to him for support or reassurance.

"Okay if I sit here?" he asked, gesturing to the couch.

"Mason, you can sit wherever you'd like. You know that."

"I thought maybe I ought to stop doing that."

"Doing what?"

"You know, doing whatever I want—at least where you're concerned." He braced his elbows on his knees. "Over the last day or so I've been thinking that I've done a lot of that."

"A lot of what?"

"You know. Doing what I thought was best. Expecting you to be okay with it."

It took everything she had not to pretend she didn't know what he meant. But he had it wrong, especially since she'd just been thinking the same thing. "Some habits are hard to break, right?" She smiled at him. "I think there will always be a part of me that idolizes you."

He winced. "I sure hope not."

"Okay, how about this, then? You've always been a good brother, and I've been glad about that."

"Was I? Even back when we both still lived at home? I think that's giving me a bit more credit than I deserve."

Boy, they were sure being honest with each other. "Okay, how's this? You were fine. Probably as good as I was to you. As good as we might have expected, don't you think?"

A line formed in between his brows. It was obvious he was concentrating on every word she was saying. "Why do you say that, Li?"

"Come on. We didn't live in a sitcom, Mason. Our parents were fine but it wasn't like Mom was Carol Brady or Dad was—" she drew a blank "—whatever dad was really great and understanding on television."

"They did the best they could."

Those six words had always been their mantra. Her and Mason's excuse for their parents never completely committing to parenthood.

But over time Liana had learned that their best had been good enough. After all, Billy had taught her that things could've been a whole lot worse. "Why are you thinking about them?"

He shrugged. "I don't know. I guess because I have Cooper."

"Cooper's perfect and you're a good father, Mason." She smiled at him. "In spite of everything, we turned out okay, right?"

That had obviously been the wrong thing to say. Mason's expression darkened. "Now you're okay."

"Mason, why are you here?"

His blue eyes, so like hers, looked at her directly. "You know why, Li. Two days ago two cops came to the shop to talk to me."

"Two of them were there?"

"Officer Olson and his father." His lips tightened. "Crazy that they're in the same profession and work together by choice. Weird, right?"

She thought it was weird that Kent's father had been

with Kent, but it wasn't like he told her much about his days. "You know I've spent time with Kent. I told you that."

"I know."

"Well, I've met his father, too. His name is Richard."

"What, they do house calls, too?" His joke sounded as brittle as his voice.

"I went to Kent's parents' house for dinner one evening." When Mason looked horrified by the news, she shook her head at him. "Stop. Richard was nice to me. Peggy, I mean, Mrs. Olson, made a really great strawberry shortcake." All of it had been nice.

"I don't know what to say about that." He patted the pocket on his shirt. It was obvious he was looking for his usual pack of cigarettes.

He was stressed.

Maybe it was time to put him out of his misery. "How about you tell me the truth about why you came over here, Mason?" Bracing herself, she brought up what she feared the most. "Are you here to yell at me? Do you hate me now?"

He froze. "For what?"

"You obviously think I told Kent to speak with you. I didn't."

Mason stared at her a moment longer before shifting. Hurt had flared in his eyes, making Liana realize that she wasn't the only one of them who had to overcome a whole lot of past ghosts. "I could never hate you. Never."

"I'm sorry."

Her brother shrugged off her apology.

"Li, the cops questioned me. For a while I think they thought I actually killed your loser husband."

She gaped at him. "You didn't?"

"No. No, I did not." He looked as puzzled as she felt. "Wait a minute. Liana, have you really thought I killed Billy? You've thought that all this time? All these years?"

"Not exactly. At first, I thought he had left me for a couple of days. Then I thought that maybe he was stuck somewhere." She shrugged. "I don't know, that maybe his dealer or somebody was forcing him to do something." Feeling foolish, she said, "I guess that was stupid."

"What about after that?"

She supposed she had to say it. "I...well, Mason, I remembered what I looked like when you saw me that day. I remembered how you took off after him and how I knew that you were going to talk to him. I knew that if you did go talk to him, he wasn't going to take anything you said well."

"We didn't have much of a conversation, Li. I meant to tell him what I really thought...but I didn't."

She stopped fidgeting and forced herself to look her brother directly in the eyes. "Mason, to tell you the truth, I was stuck. No matter how much Billy and I didn't like each other or how much neither of us wanted to be married, I knew he wasn't going to let me divorce him. I also knew that I wasn't going to survive too many of those beatings."

She lifted her chin. "So God help me, I hoped and prayed that you did kill him. Because then I would be free. And I decided that if I never spoke of it, if I never asked you, then I'd never have to actually know what happened," she finished, her voice almost a whisper. "I'm sorry."

He looked devastated, but not exactly surprised. "I went to see Billy. I lied years ago about that. I told the cops that I never talked to him, but I did."

"What did you do?"

"When I first found him, he was with his buddies. So I waited around until he was alone."

"And?"

Mason shrugged. "And what do you think? I could tell he was hopped up on something. No way were we going to have any kind of conversation…so I told him that he should stop hitting you. And then I hit him."

"Really?"

He looked down at his right hand that was fisted on his lap. "I'm not proud of myself, but he deserved it. Which is why, when he attempted to hit me back, I hit him a couple more times." He bit his bottom lip. "To be honest with you, Liana, I did my best to hurt him so bad that he'd think twice about touching you again."

"Oh, Mason."

"I didn't kill him, Liana. When I left Billy, he was lying on the ground, his nose bleeding and moaning like he'd gotten so soft, he'd never done all those two-a-days next to me back in high school."

"What did you think happened to him?"

His expression turned blank. "By the time you told me he'd been missing for a couple of days, I was pretty sure that someone else killed him."

"I wonder who it could have been." Then she realized that her brother didn't look confused at all. "Who killed Billy, Mason?"

"That, I'm not going to say."

She couldn't believe Mason had come over just to

leave it at that. Letting her frustration fly, she said, "Mason, whoever killed him broke his neck and hand-cuffed him and tossed him in a ravine."

"Do you think I care about that? I don't."

"Then how about this. Haven't we kept enough se-crets?"

"You aren't wrong. The pair of us really have kept too much too quiet. It's a bad habit. A dangerous one."

"Then don't you think it's time we stopped? I de-serve to know."

For a minute she thought he was going to give in. But then he shook his head. "Sorry. There are some things... well, some things you never need to hear from me and this is one of them."

It was all she could do not to roll her eyes. "Aren't you going to finish that thought and tell me that one day I'm going to thank you?"

He didn't crack a smile. "Liana, one day you're going to thank me for this. I promise." Before she could de-bate that, Mason stepped forward and kissed her brow. "Sorry, but I gotta run. Call Jeanie soon and set up din-ner or something. I want to see more of you."

Realizing that it would do no good to argue with him, she said, "I will." Walking him to the door, she added, "I love you, Mason, and I know you love me, too."

His expression cleared. "Never doubt that, Li. You're my kid sister. I'll always love you." Looking awkward, he added, "So I'll um... I'll see you later. Now go on and paint."

She smiled as she closed the door. This was why God gave people siblings, she decided. Everyone needed someone in their life who told them what they really thought out of love. She didn't always agree with Mason, but she knew he loved her and she loved him back.

No, everything between them wasn't perfect. But what they had was enough.

Chapter Twenty-Six

Down in the cold-case basement, sitting at his bare-bones cubicle across the room from Sergeant Crier, Kent knew it was time to close the Billy Mann case.

He even knew how he was going to do it. Now, it was just a matter of when. It was going to require finesse when it came to the person he needed to speak with, for a variety of reasons. And because of that, he'd been working on his notes and reviewing his options for two hours. The last thing he wanted was to ruin the case because he was in a rush.

No, the last thing he wanted to do was hurt Liana by overlooking some detail and therefore causing her more harm.

"You've sure been staring at the same five pages for a while," the sergeant said. "They giving you fits?"

Kent turned around to face his boss. "No. Not really. I think I'm more afraid of missing something obvious."

"Do you want to talk about it?"

It had taken Kent four months to realize a couple of things about the cranky, curmudgeonly sergeant. The first was that the man's bark, while loud and pointed, really was worse than his bite. The next was that his first name was Vincent, which he hated. The third was the most important. The man cared passionately about these cold-case files, and he in no way thought of any officer's time on the tasks to be anything but important and valued police work.

All that was why Kent answered him as honestly as he could. "Thanks, but I think I need to do this on my own. I mean, as much as I can."

"I'm going to tell you something, but I don't want you to take it the wrong way."

"Okay…"

Sergeant Crier looked at him intently. "From the time you started on the Mann case, I've noticed something different about you. Something better."

The younger version of Kent might have been offended. But the person he was now was intrigued. "How so?"

"I think you care more now. It shows."

That took Kent off guard. "I've always cared."

Crier continued to look him in the eye. "Maybe you did and you just looked like you didn't—or that was my perspective. What I'm trying to say is that while I might not have been real glad to have you down here in the basement at first, I sure am glad about it now."

"Thank you, Sergeant."

The older man shrugged off the thanks like it embarrassed him. "I know your goal is to get back in the detective unit, but if you ever change your mind about these files down here, I'd be real glad to put in a good word for you to take over for me one day."

"Take over? Are you already thinking about retirement?"

"I've been working for this police department twenty-five years, and that's after I put in my five years to the army. I'm starting to think it might be nice to wear my own clothes for a spell."

"I can see that, Sarge." Clearing his throat, he added, "And Crier, I'll think about what you said. You're right. I came here thinking that I needed to prove myself and then get out. But after working on Billy Mann's case, I have a new appreciation for it. Helping to solve his murder would mean a lot to me."

Sergeant Crier nodded in acknowledgment. "I've always thought that someone needed to speak for these victims. Someone who would give them the dignity they deserve."

"Yes, sir."

"Now, about your case."

"Yes?"

"Stop overthinking it. You've got this. I promise."

"Yes, sir." Just as Kent was about to tell Crier that he appreciated his belief in him, the sergeant's phone buzzed.

"Yeah?" he barked into the receiver. "Hmm?" He glanced at Kent. "Okay, then. Send him down." When he hung up, Crier almost smiled. "You've got some company coming."

"Who?"

"A man by the name of Mason Kelly. Ring a bell?"

"Oh yeah." That was exactly the one person he needed to see. "Do you mind if I take him to the conference room?"

"You work here, too, Olson."

Grinning, he walked to the elevator just as it opened,

revealing Mason Kelly in a pair of jeans, clean T-shirt and a pensive expression.

"Mason, good to see you," he said as he held out his hand.

"Thanks, I think." After shaking it, Mason looked around the area, taking in the cement walls, long strips of fluorescent lights lining the center of the ceiling and the industrial-grade dark blue carpet. "So this is where you work?"

"Yeah."

"It feels like the morgue. Are there any windows around?"

"Nope."

"Huh."

Kent chuckled as Mason was obviously trying hard to not disparage the basement any more than he already had. "It's taken some getting used to, but it ain't too bad."

"I'll take your word for it."

"I thought we could meet in the conference room. It's at the end of the hall. Someone tried to make it seem a little more livable a few years back."

Leading him into the space, Kent realized that the room really was a step up from the rest of the cold-case rooms. There was real carpet in a soft beige, the walls had been drywalled and painted a creamy white and the furniture was wood instead of metal.

"Have a seat," he said, gesturing to one of the eight padded chairs surrounding the table.

After Mason sat down, Kent sat across from him. "I just realized that I didn't bring in a recorder or any paper. Do you need me to take notes?"

"I don't think so. But you can go get it if you want."

Kent debated before deciding against it. He needed to do what Crier had suggested and trust his gut. And his gut was telling him that Mason Kelly was a nervous wreck and that there was a very good chance he'd take off if Kent gave him much time to actually think about what he was going to say.

"I'll be okay," he replied. "If we start to talk and I think I'm going to miss something I'll go get some paper. Sound good?"

"Yeah. That's fine with me." Mason shifted uncomfortably in his chair. Cracked his neck. Then stared back at Kent. "Are you going to start asking me questions?"

"I could, but since I'm not exactly sure what you came to talk to me about, I'm afraid you're going to have to get us started."

"Fine." He took a breath, then blurted, "I know you're seeing my sister. Even though you're a cop, I really can't blame her for liking you. I mean, you're the complete opposite of Billy."

Since that wasn't exactly hard to be, Kent figured it was pretty slim praise. "Thanks," he said drily.

"Liana seeing you, together with Billy's body being found and the investigation…well, it's made me have to deal with some things I had gotten good at pretending didn't happen."

"Things like what?"

"Things like I'm pretty sure our father killed Billy."

The statement hung heavy between them. No, it was more like Mason's statement flitted between them like a nervous hummingbird. Busy and full of consequences that were hard to completely nail down.

Mason grunted as he shifted yet again. "Aren't you going to say something?"

"I am. I was just attempting to weigh my words. I'm trying to get better about not saying stupid stuff."

Looking amused, Mason asked, "How's that going for you?"

"With Liana, pretty good. With you, maybe not so much." Waiting a second, giving Mason a moment to compose himself and maybe realize that Kent was giving himself a hard time rather than the other man, he said, "Maybe you could tell me about why you think your father, uh, killed Billy."

"Because we were all starting to realize that Billy was beating up my sister something awful."

"It's my understanding that he did that for a while. Maybe years."

Mason visibly winced. "I guess you think I'm worthless, huh? I mean, what kind of man who loves his sister would allow that to happen?"

"You tell me."

"The thing is that I knew Billy from back in high school. He wasn't someone I'd count as a close friend, but we'd been on the football team together." He glanced at Kent. "Did you play?"

"I played baseball and soccer."

"Oh." He cleared his throat. "Well, football and team building was big at our school. Our coach pretty much made us believe that all the guys on our team were family. We were responsible for each other." He looked just above Kent's shoulder. "You know, like if someone needed to study for a test so they could pass it and play on Friday night, we weren't supposed to encourage him to blow it off. Things like that."

"I understand."

"Yeah. So Billy was okay. We weren't really close

but all of my friends thought he was cool. Later, when he started asking after my sister, I actually thought it was a good thing."

"Liana told me she was the artsy girl."

"She was that. And timid. And kind of mousy, if you want to know the truth." Looking like he thought Kent was going to yell at him for saying it, he added quickly, "I know it's hard to see that now. She's real pretty and real talented. But back then? Years ago? Well, she was different, I guess."

"I reckon we were all different years ago."

Mason seemed to consider that for a moment. "I guess that's true." He shifted again. Felt in his pocket for a cigarette. When he found it empty, he cracked his knuckles.

Finally, he spoke again. "So…at first, Liana seemed happy with Billy. And because she wasn't just sitting by herself painting stuff that looked like giant blobs, we were all glad about that. I mean, me and Jeanie."

"Your parents weren't?"

"By then my mom was pretty sick and my dad was just stressing about work and bills. He didn't want to deal with Li, if you want to know the truth. 'Course, he never really had."

"What changed?"

"What do you mean?"

"I mean, how did your father go from not really wanting to deal with Liana to murdering her husband?"

Mason took a moment, obviously wanting to convey the past in a clear, concise way. "After they were married two years, Liana started avoiding all of us. Then Mom died and Liana came over with me to clean up her stuff."

Everything about Mason seemed to harden. "That was the first time I saw the bruises. It wasn't just one, either. There were faded marks, cuts. She'd lost weight. She didn't want to talk about any of it but I kept pressing her."

"How did Liana respond?"

"How do you think? I went about it all the wrong way." He closed his eyes. "I sound so concerned, right? I mean, what was I thinking? I actually told her that I needed to know who had hurt her. Like I didn't think it could've been her husband."

"Did she tell you it was Billy?"

"No. She kept saying that it wasn't any of my business and that there wasn't anything I could do, anyway."

"Then what happened?"

"Billy stopped by and he looked really bad. Like he was on something. He was talking about some new buddies of his and how he was going to finally make something of himself." Mason waved a hand. "Crazy talk."

"And?"

"And my dad heard. And it was as if he finally saw the same thing I did. We took a good long look at Liana and realized that not only was she getting abused, we were letting it happen. So when Liana went to the bathroom to wash up, I told Billy that he needed to start taking care of her better."

"What did he say to that?"

Mason scoffed. "What do you think Billy said? He said that Liana was fine and that it wasn't any of our business, anyway, because she was his wife."

"What did your father say to that?" Kent prodded.

"Dad started saying how he'd trusted Billy to look after her. He started talking about marriage vows and

God and how Billy had promised to honor her. But that's when Billy laughed."

"He laughed?" Honestly, Kent could feel his blood pressure rise.

"Oh yeah. I couldn't believe it. He said we were too much, suddenly acting like we cared about her. And that's when he directly looked my father in the eye and said that if he was all that concerned about his daughter, where had he been when we were all in high school? Where had my mom and dad been back in eighth grade when girls had been teasing her—no, *bullying* her—about how she didn't fit in?"

"Wow."

Mason leaned back in his chair. "I know, right? That drug-addicted, wife-beating loser had not only been watching Liana for years, he'd been aware of our neglect." His voice turned hoarse. "He'd known that no one in her house had ever really put themselves out there for her. Which was why he didn't understand why Dad gave a flip about her now."

"That had to hurt to hear."

"Of course it did, but it wasn't anything I hadn't told myself already. I mean, a guy can only believe so many of the lies he tells himself before he realizes that they don't mean a thing."

"What does that conversation have to do with Billy's death? You said it took place two years before he died, right?"

Mason nodded. "After that Dad and I tried to check on Liana more often. I mean, at least I did." His voice quieted. "But it was too late to suddenly act like we really cared. Liana didn't trust either of us enough to seek help. She even became more withdrawn. She wouldn't return phone calls, wouldn't come over when we invited her for dinner."

"What happened after you saw Billy with his friends, Mason?"

"I... I actually did end up talking to Billy. When he was alone. I told him to stop hurting Liana. And I might have hit him a couple of times."

"Did you kill him after all?"

"No. I promise I didn't. I left him on the ground and went home. But my father was at my house with Jeanie. She'd invited him over for supper." He took a deep breath. "Of course, as soon as Jeanie saw my knuckles, she freaked out until I told her what happened."

"And then?"

"And I realized then that my dad had taken off," he said slowly. "And I had a pretty good idea where he went."

Kent raised his eyebrows. "But you didn't do a thing about it? You didn't follow him?"

"No." Mason's expression hardened. "Maybe there was a part of me that thought Dad should've stepped in already, that it was his turn to try to help Liana." He rolled his eyes. "Or maybe I just didn't want to know what he did."

"You didn't feel like you should do or say anything when you realized that your brother-in-law was missing?"

"If you want me to suddenly act remorseful about that, you're gonna have to wait a long time. Sorry, but I can't do it." He shrugged. "The fact of it was that I was glad nobody was hitting her anymore. Plus, we all thought that Billy had just run off. So I waited. And then... I don't know. Those first few days turned into a week, then a month, then several months, and all of us breathed a sigh of relief. At last, Billy Mann was gone—and there wasn't a single one of us who cared where he was."

"Do you have proof that your father was involved?"

"When I cleaned out the attic of my parents' house after Dad died, I found a gun that I hadn't known he owned. Maybe there's something there?"

Kent spoke with Mason for a few more minutes, but since he and his father had come to mostly the same conclusion, he didn't keep him much longer.

Only when he was walking up the stairs did Mason look worried. "Have I just messed up everything with you and Liana?"

For some reason, having his suspect worry about his love life felt fitting. That was the kind of case this had been—a tangled mess of knots and lies and frayed emotions. "If Liana is upset with me…well, that's on me, not you."

"Hey, listen. Don't give up on her. As hard as the truth is to hear sometimes, I think she'd agree that lies are harder to live with," Mason said.

Kent was certain that was the best advice he'd heard all day. "I'll be in touch," he said. "Thank you for coming in and telling me the rest of the story."

After Mason was long gone, Kent walked back toward the cold-case room. He needed to write down his notes, confer with Sergeant Crier and then get up the nerve to give Liana a call.

No, he needed to see her. And he needed to see her as soon as possible.

Chapter Twenty-Seven

The first thing Kent had done after he'd walked inside her house was give her a hug. Soon after, he'd taken her hand, sat next to her on the couch and described how he believed her father had killed her husband. Then, as if he'd had a need to heighten that awful moment, Kent explained how Mason had shown up at the station house just a few hours earlier and told him all of this.

Included in his speech was the fact that Liana's father had hidden the murder weapon in his attic this whole time. Mason had discovered it after their father had died but kept it a secret. Because he hadn't known *for sure* that that was why his father owned a gun no one knew he had and then stored it in a box in his attic.

Throughout the whole conversation, Liana had sat there stiff and mute. Like a wooden doll. She'd been so stunned, it had been almost impossible to do anything besides stare at Kent and wonder what he was going to say next. The whole situation didn't even seem real.

Or maybe it was just that it was so different from what she'd imagined had happened. Somehow, learning her father had killed Billy and then hidden the murder weapon was very different from Mason accosting Billy in a fit of rage.

She supposed they really were two different scenarios. One was premeditated, while the other was not.

While Kent continued his report, giving her all kinds of details and facts she didn't care too much about, Liana drew inward. Was she more relieved that Mason was innocent or upset that her father took another life? For that matter, how culpable was she? Though she hadn't attacked Billy, killed him or been anywhere near him when the event had occurred, she'd been the reason for it.

Why had she stayed so quiet all this time? How had she been okay with keeping all her suspicions to herself?

Ten minutes later, when Kent finished his speech at long last, he drew a breath. "Are you okay?" he asked.

"I'm not really sure."

He continued to eye her warily. "I think that's understandable. Your world has been turned upside down."

Was it, though? So many thoughts were running through her brain, it was hard to keep them organized. "I'm relieved to finally know the truth," she said at last. "Maybe I'm feeling stunned, too. I never imagined my father would have done a thing like that…or even that Mason would tell it to you instead of me."

"I think they were trying to protect you. Your father by going after Billy and your brother by never mentioning that day."

She supposed they were. But had she actually been protected all this time? All she remembered at the moment was being afraid of Billy's return and being suspected of his murder.

Kent stood up. "Liana, I've hoped and prayed for closure on this case for so many reasons. Some have been selfish, some have been professional, some have been for Billy." He paused, then added, "But most of all, as we've gotten to know each other, I've prayed that solving the case would give you some much-needed closure. I can't help but think that one day you'll feel more at peace."

"What is going to happen to my father? I mean, to his memory?"

"Well, we'll run some tests to see if we can determine that the weapon was used in the murder. But even if it has been, I don't know if we'll ever be able to say with a hundred percent certainty that your father was the one who fired the shot. He died years ago."

"And Mason? Will he be charged for anything?"

He shook his head. "No, Liana. A lot of people talk to friends and loved ones about things that upset them. That doesn't mean they're responsible for other people's actions. Besides, years ago, when Officer Grune did the initial investigation, Mason had alibis for the evening Billy went missing as well as the following two days. Both my sergeant and I will count this case as closed."

She figured everything he was saying made sense, but it also seemed almost too convenient.

"Thank you for coming over to tell me," she said formally. "I appreciate it."

His eyebrows rose. "*Of course* I wanted to be the one to tell you the news. But Li, we both know that isn't the only reason I'm here. Would you like me to make you some tea or something? Can we talk some more?"

She didn't want to talk to him about the case or about the report. She really didn't want to hear him say how relieved he was because he was on his way out of the cold-case division.

No, all she wanted at the moment was some space from him. "Kent, please don't take this the wrong way, but I'd like to be alone."

Hurt flared in his expression before he quickly composed himself. "Are you sure?" He reached for her phone. "Want me to call your brother or sister-in-law?"

She pulled her cell from his reach. "I can't imagine anything worse than you giving Mason a call right now."

"You're upset."

"I am," she admitted. "Though I know none of this is your fault. I know you were just doing your job."

"I had to solve it, Liana. I had to do my job. Not only was it necessary for you and for the department, it was also important for me and my reputation."

"I realize that." Looking down at her feet, she murmured, "I'm upset about a lot of things. Not just you. Actually, I think I'm most upset with myself."

"Why is that? Liana, you didn't do anything wrong. You were as much of a victim as Billy was."

"That's where you're mistaken," she said, her voice shaking. "There were a lot of opportunities for me to stop what was happening. I could have left him or called the police or gone to a shelter or let Mason help me. Instead, I did what I always did and kept everything hidden away."

"It's easy to go back and look at mistakes and blame yourself. I've done that plenty of times myself. But it doesn't help, especially if you aren't to blame." He took a deep breath. "Liana, you didn't cause his death. Just like you didn't deserve Billy's treatment of you."

Liana was sure Kent believed every word he said. However, she wasn't sure if she believed them. Getting to her feet, she said, "Thank you for letting me know in person."

"I love you, Liana. I'm not just falling in love with you. Not just infatuated. I'm *in* love. I want to spend the rest of my life with you."

She blinked, almost hating him for telling her something so perfect practically two minutes after giving her some of the worst news of her life.

Standing up, she pointed to the door. "Could you see yourself out?"

He blinked as hurt seemed to infuse every one of his features. "That's it? That's all you're going to say?"

"I'm sorry, but that's all I have to give right now."

It was obvious that he didn't want to leave. For a moment she didn't think he was going to, but then he walked to the door. "Lock it behind me, okay? And when I call you later, please pick up. If you don't, I'm going to come back over here. I have to know you're safe."

She nodded. And only breathed deeply after he'd left.

And then she cried for her father and Mason and Billy and for herself. And maybe she cried for Kent, too.

Because some situations were so bad, there was plenty of pain to go around.

Chapter Twenty-Eight

Two weeks later

Two days after Kent had come over and she had practically pushed him out of her house, Liana decided to make some changes in her life. It was time to quit being afraid and doubting herself. Most of all, she realized that she needed to stop looking backward. She had a lot of skills, a God-given talent and a great support system now. No matter how her life used to be, she wasn't the same woman she'd once been.

The very next morning she went to the diner early and gave Gabe and Viv her two weeks' notice.

But instead of granting her that time, Viv had hugged her and sent her on her way. It seemed that there were a couple of girls who had been begging for more hours and Viv had been delaying giving it to them until Liana had finally come to the realization that she had other things to do besides wait tables.

Suddenly, after years of juggling so much with so little, Liana had free time. She started going for more walks and stopping by Martha and Sol's house for cups of coffee. She also tried to get excited about her future. Now she had time to paint as much as she wanted. She also had enough money in the bank to do a lot of things she'd only dreamed about.

But ironically, instead of being thrilled about that, all she felt was adrift. Her painting, which had always been her source of happiness and her outlet for all of her pain, had suddenly become her vocation. Her job.

Worse, she feared she wasn't even doing a very good job with them. Now, when she looked at her paintings, all she noticed was their flaws. Maybe they were blotches all along and she just hadn't realized it?

She was staring at her latest work, titled simply *Roses Bloom*, when she received a text and the doorbell rang at the same time.

Glad to put down her paintbrush, she hurried to the door and glanced out the window. And laughed for the first time in days.

Angel and Viv were standing on her stoop, still dressed in their waitress uniforms. Angel was also holding a whole pie.

Liana hurried to let them in. "This is a nice surprise!" she exclaimed as she hugged each of them. "I'm so glad to see you both."

After Viv seemed to study her from top to bottom, she led the way inside. "I'm so glad to see you, too, sweetheart. Though I told Angel that we needed to call first. I'm sorry we didn't."

"I figured she was right," Angel said with a laugh. "That's why I texted you when we got to the door."

Liana held up the phone. "I got it. Thanks."

"Are we interrupting?" Viv motioned to her outfit, which was comprised of old, black-turned-to-gray threadbare leggings, her white Keds she'd waitressed in and her favorite painting T-shirt, which was stained with about a dozen different colors. She didn't have a bit of makeup on and hadn't washed her hair in two days.

"I was painting, but obviously, I think I needed a break."

Angel didn't even attempt to hide her dismay at Liana's appearance. "What you need is a shower, girl."

"I know." She sighed. "I'm a mess, in more ways than one."

Angel held up the pie. "It sounds like this pie didn't come a moment too soon. Where's the kitchen?"

"Straight ahead." When Angel strode forward, Liana trotted to keep up. "What kind of pie is that?"

"What kind do you think? Gabe's famous coconut cream pie," Viv said. "He made it especially for you."

The thought of Gabe taking the time to make her a pie brought tears to her eyes. "That's the sweetest thing."

"We miss you," Viv said softly. "Now, we're going to eat, but first I want to see these paintings of yours."

"I'll be happy to show them to you. But first, I'll put on a pot of coffee," Liana said.

Just as she put in the grounds, Angel groaned. "Liana, what in the world is going on with this sink of yours?"

She turned to get a good look at it. "What's wrong?"

"What's wrong is that it's filled to the brim with dirty dishes."

Viv picked up a dishrag and wrinkled her nose. "This is gross. Where are your clean dishcloths?"

"In the cabinet under the sink." When she saw Viv was about to grab one, Liana called out, "Don't you dare start cleaning!"

"Someone has to," Angel said. "I'm surprised you have any clean plates at all."

"I have a couple left." At least, she hoped she did. While she filled up the coffee carafe with water, her girlfriends made rude comments about the state of her range. "I know, I know. But pretend you don't see my mess. Y'all are my guests."

"I'm starting to feel less like an uninvited guest and more like a woman on a mission of mercy," Angel said. "Girl, you're in a sorry state."

After closing the coffeemaker's lid, she pressed Brew. "The coffee's brewing now. Are you ready to see my studio?"

"Of course," Viv said. "Lead the way, Li."

With a bit of trepidation, she walked them down the hall, wondering what they'd think of her work…especially her newest piece, which was so different from a lot of other things she'd made in the past.

Thankfully, the door was closed. "Just warning you, it's a mess in here, too."

"I wouldn't have expected anything less," Viv said. "Stop stalling and let us in."

"Okay." She took a breath and motioned them in.

"Oh!" Angel exclaimed. "Oh, wow. Viv, come look at this thing."

Liana watched them both stare up at *Roses Bloom*. She couldn't read their expressions. "Um, I'm still working on it. Careful, now. It's still wet and those oils don't come off clothes easily."

Angel was intently studying her painting. "Are these…flowers?"

Liana nodded. "I'm surprised you can tell."

"It looks the way flowers look when you get a

bouquet and you're so excited that you start crying," Viv said.

Angel nodded. "That's it to a T. It's the way roses look through tears." She grinned. "Listen to me, sounding just like a fancy art critic. How did I do?"

Liana felt like crying. "Usually, I tell people that my paintings depict whatever they want them to be, but you're exactly right. It's roses through a sheet of tears."

"I love it," Angel said sincerely. "This is the most beautiful thing I've ever seen."

Viv pulled her into a hug. "You, Liana Mann, have a gift. And you should not be doing anything but standing in here in this dirty room in those dirty clothes and painting things like this."

And that was when she lost it. She started crying. "I don't know what to do."

"How come? Don't you have everything you ever wanted?"

That caught Liana off guard, but she realized that Angel was right. Everything she had secretly ever wanted had come to life. Billy was no longer hurting her. He was no longer missing. His murder was solved.

She'd found an incredible man who'd told her he loved her. And he wanted her just how she was.

She'd quit her job at the diner because she could now afford to paint full-time.

So why was she such a mess?

"I don't know if I have everything I ever wanted. I thought I did, but maybe I'm hard to please."

"You aren't," Angel pronounced. "Your trouble is that you've been living that life of Job."

Liana gaped at her. "Job, like in the Bible?"

"Ah, yeah." Angel folded her arms over her chest.

"Here's the thing, Liana. Job had a lot of trials and a grumpy wife. But he was also missing something really important. It was so important that he hardly survived."

"What was that?"

"Hope, girl." Angel looked at her carefully. "Don't you know all about the group of threes?"

"I have no idea what you're talking about."

Angel exhaled like she was a put-upon middle school teacher. "Liana, it goes like this. You can go through a lot and still survive. But you can only go about three weeks without food, three days without water, three minutes without air…and only three seconds without hope."

"Only three seconds without hope," she echoed.

"Good. You're listening. Liana girl, you need to start looking at the future instead of the past. You need to grasp that hope and hold on tight."

"And if I do?" she asked, still afraid to believe that things could get brighter.

Angel smiled sweetly. "If you do, then everything is going to be just fine."

Later, after the three of them had consumed almost the whole pie and cleaned her kitchen together, and then Liana had sent them on their way with promises of getting together soon… Liana finally reached out to two more of the people in her life whom she loved dearly.

Keeping it simple, she texted Mason and told him that she'd finally like to take him up on his invitation to dinner.

Then she gathered her courage and texted Kent. The message wasn't long but it was to the point.

I just want you to know that I love you.

It wasn't much, but it was a start.

And when her phone buzzed right back with responses from not just one of the men but both...she
smiled.

Mason had thrown out a couple of dates, which made
her laugh.

But Kent's note? Well, it made everything in her life
seem like it was going to be okay after all.

I love you, too.

Warmth and happiness infused her, feelings that
were almost unfamiliar, they had been absent for so
long.

She'd found hope again. At last.

Chapter Twenty-Nine

One week later

The ceremony had been short and with only a few members of the department present, but that had been by Kent's request, not because his captain hadn't considered his accomplishment to be noteworthy.

But when Kent had stood next to Sergeant Crier in front of Captain Velasquez, he'd never been more proud, especially when he'd seen the look of joy in his father's eyes.

"Officer Olson, for your efforts to uncover the real story in the Billy Mann murder, and for closing the cold case in an efficient and thorough manner, I present to you this commendation." He handed him a certificate in a small leather folder. "Thank you for a job well-done."

"Thank you, sir," Kent said as he shook his hand.

The captain said a few more words, but they were a blur to Kent. Though he was proud of his work, he wasn't craving either the recognition of his captain or congratulatory words from men like Jackson and some of his other longtime coworkers.

Actually, ever since he'd been sent down to the cold-case files, all he'd ever wanted was to get out of there. Until now. Now he was eager to get back to his desk and away from the politics that the rest of the precinct seemed to buzz with.

After he spoke a few words to the captain, both his father and Sergeant Crier approached him.

"Congratulations, Officer Olson," his sergeant said. "It was a job well-done."

"I appreciate your help and patience with me, sir. Yours, too, Dad."

"I'm proud of you, son," his father said as he shook his hand.

"Thank you, Dad."

"Did I hear right that you have accepted Sergeant Crier's offer?" Dad said with a grin.

Sharing a look with Crier, Kent nodded. "You did. Within the year, I plan on being the sergeant in charge while this guy goes fishing every day."

"Some days that day can't get here soon enough," the sergeant grumbled.

"Make that two of us," his father announced. "I'll be retiring at the end of the year, too."

"Dad, really?"

"It's time. Past time, really. I realized when I visited Joe and those guys the other day that a lot of time has passed. A lot of years. I'm ready to spend more time with your mother and relax more, especially since I've passed the baton on to my son."

Kent couldn't believe it, but everything his father said made sense. "I'll miss knowing that you're here."

"Oh, I'll still be there for you, Kent. But I promise you're going to be just fine." He rested his hand on

Kent's arm. "Better than that, I think." Turning to the sergeant, he said, "We need to make plans to go out to the lake soon."

Crier grinned. "Those bass won't stand a chance."

Later that night Kent called Liana. Ever since she'd sent her text and he'd told her he loved her back, they were making strides in their relationship. They'd started seeing each other every couple of days and calling and texting several times a day.

Liana had told him about Angel and Viv's visit, along with the hours she'd spent with Mason. It looked like everyone was healing and moving forward.

"So how did your painting go today?" he asked after they exchanged greetings.

"It went." She chuckled. "I worked at home for a couple of hours before going with Serena to deliver two of my paintings to a buyer's home."

He smiled. She'd told him that delivering paintings was now one of her favorite things to do. "How did it go?"

"You know what? It went great. We hung the canvases next to each other in their entryway. They looked amazing."

"I hope you took some pictures of them hanging up."

"I think I took one or two. Or maybe ten," she teased. "I'll show them to you next time we see each other. Now, tell me how your big awards ceremony was."

"It lasted all of ten minutes, but it was great. My dad was there, and Sergeant Crier, too. They seemed very pleased."

"It's nice for your hard work to be recognized, Kent. I'm proud of you."

That meant a lot, especially given how much this case had cost her. "So when can I see you? Tomorrow?"

"So soon? I'm planning to go to church and lunch with you and your parents on Sunday."

"Sunday isn't soon enough. How about we spend tomorrow together? We'll go for a walk on the bike trail."

"That sounds perfect, Kent."

Now that their plans were finalized he settled in to talk with her some more, which they did for the next hour, not a bit of it too serious or important. But that was what they'd needed, he realized. They needed time to simply get to know each other. Time to fill in all the gaps that the tumultuous beginning of their relationship hadn't allowed them to explore.

Time to fall in *like* the way they'd fallen in love.

Chapter Thirty

Two months later

"What a difference two months makes," Kent teased.

Looking at her dark navy dress and matching handbag, Liana had to admit that she agreed completely. Two weeks ago Serena had called in a panic, asking if she would please, please attend another showing at Gallery One.

Liana had hemmed and hawed a bit, but mainly out of habit. Now that she'd met a couple of her buyers in person, Liana was starting to realize that she needed this connection to them as much as she needed her art. The buyers she'd met seemed to provide a link that she hadn't even realized had been missing. Though she still painted her bold abstracts according to wherever her mood took her, she also would sometimes imagine how they'd look in a home or business. It made her feel as if her new profession wasn't quite as solitary as she'd once believed it was.

So of course she'd said yes to Serena. When she asked Kent if he wouldn't mind attending another show-

ing, he said he'd be happy to go…if she'd invite Viv, Gabe and Angel, as well.

Of course, when she'd done that, Angel had insisted a fancy gallery party needed a fancy party dress. The two of them had ended up spending an afternoon at Kenwood Mall in Cincinnati, trying on dozens of gorgeous dresses. It had been so much fun, Liana had bought two dresses for herself and Angel's dress, too. It made her so happy to be able to do something for the woman who had been so encouraging.

Looking down at her navy dress, Liana had to admit that it was a giant step up from her previous waiter look.

Returning her attention back to Kent, she said, "Sometimes, when I think of how blessed I am, I get a little dizzy. It's just so hard to believe."

"Your career is pretty amazing, but you deserve all of your accolades. You work hard and you're talented. I'm proud of you, honey."

"I wasn't just talking about my art. I was talking about us."

"Well, in that case? You're exactly right. We are blessed." He reached down and kissed her brow. "Incredibly blessed."

She beamed at him, thinking how far they'd come over the past two months. They'd gone from texts, calls and occasional dates to trying to spend time with each other every day. Well, as much as Kent's job allowed. He'd already solved another case and was now working on two more concurrently.

She was learning how much solving these *forgotten* cases meant to him. He really felt as if he was making a difference in peoples' lives. And, since she knew that to be true, she was as supportive as she could be.

Yes, they really had gone a long way from being just friends to their status now as an official couple.

"Here we are," Kent said as he pulled into Gallery One's parking lot. As he backed into the spot that Serena had left open for them, he pointed at the windows of the gallery. "And just like last time, your paintings look incredible."

"They really do." Glancing through the large plate-glass windows, she saw five of her biggest paintings on one wall. And in the entryway was *Roses Bloom*, her pride and joy. Serena's, too. Serena had cried when she'd seen it.

After he helped her out of the car, he said, "So what have you decided to do? Chat or give a speech?"

"Chat, of course. I might have come a long way, but I'm not ready to go crazy and start speaking in front of crowds!"

He chuckled as he opened the door. "Maybe it's time to go a little crazy," he murmured.

She turned to him with a puzzled frown. "What did you say?"

"Turn around, Liana."

"What? Why?" she asked as he practically turned her body himself.

Just as all of their friends appeared out of hiding in one fell swoop.

"Surprise!" they chorused.

Liana gasped as she placed her hand on her chest. "What in the world?" Her eyes darted from Kent's parents to Viv, Gabe and Angel, to Jeanie and Mason to about a dozen of Kent's friends and acquaintances from work.

As they all started laughing from her shock, she reached for Kent's hand. "What is going on?" she whispered.

Grinning, he replied, "Well, it's a party for your paintings, because you've been way too secretive about them all."

"Oh my gosh. Oh, I better go thank Serena!"

"Hold on, Li. It's um, also another type of party."

"What?" She was starting to realize that the whole room had gone quiet and everyone was staring at them. "Kent," she whispered again, "what is going on?"

He kissed her forehead. "Trust me?"

"Always."

He knelt down on one knee. "Liana, you know how much I love you. You know how proud I am. You even know how I don't care that practically all of your clothes are splattered with paint. You've changed my life and given me hope and a future. My only goal in life is to try to make you happy. Will you marry me?"

Biting her lip, she nodded. "Oh yes."

He stood up, wrapped his arms around her and kissed her. Even though everyone was whistling and cheering, she closed her eyes and ignored them all as he deepened the kiss. All she cared about was this moment with Kent.

"Come on, Kent. Let her breathe!" Mason called out.

With everyone laughing, including both of them— though she was pretty sure her face would never stop being bright red—Kent linked his fingers in hers and turned so they could face everyone. All their friends and family and people who had been through some of their darkest days were now standing with them in the light.

Wrapping an arm around her shoulders, Kent said, "Everyone, please come say hi to my beautiful and talented fiancée, Liana."

When she heard the clapping, Liana felt a lump form

in her throat. This time the clapping was for them and the happiness they'd found in spite of the greatest odds.

And they were all clapping to celebrate the fact that happily-ever-afters really did still exist. For everyone.

Even for Liana and Kent.

* * * * *